THE CROWN IS MINE

Takeover Season

Part III

THE CROWN IS MINE

Takeover Season

Part III

Warren Holloway

Table of Contents

Chapter 1

For the last three months, the FBI has shuffled TK, Suga Baby, Red Rain, and Little Ki Ki around to multiple federal holding facilities. To insure they never got comfortable. Also to shake them up mentally and emotionally, keeping them stressed about their charges. Making them wonder how they got infiltrated? Where this information came from that took them down, especially running a tight organization.

Karin on the other hand, was released a few days after their arrest. Little Ki Ki made the FBI aware she knew nothing of their day to day criminal life style. The FBI didn't need her to assume responsibility. She was going to be released anyway. The FBI's main interest is TK, Suga Baby, Red Rain and Little Ki Ki.

Suga Baby was charged with trafficking, attempted homicide on a police officer, homicide for killing Four-Five. They still didn't know TK was the other person present even with their looming suspicions, with them all being arrested together. The FBI will prosecute Suga Baby first, before allowing Pennsylvania to take her. Red Rain was charged with the R. I. C. O. Act, along with attempted homicide on a police officer. Atlanta Police Department will get her once the feds are done with her and Little Ki Ki, who also was hit with the R. I. C. O. Act, being the sole supplier of the Northeast, and some of the Midwest. Suga Baby didn't have a bail, because of her homicide. TK's bail was set at twenty five million. The judge did this to assure this all cash bail would not be made, especially with him being the head of this organization, with La Vieja being murdered in cold blood, before the feds were able to apprehend her. Even La Vieja knew her reign, when it came to an end, it would be violent, she wouldn't have had it any other way. Red Rain's bail is two million cash bond. Even if she posted bail, she would be sent to Georgia for the attempted homicide on the police officer, from the day her and Suga Baby was shooting it out with Detective Wilson and his partner Detective Packard, trying to evade capture from them. Fearing the worst for her baby, being apart from TK Junior, never having a chance to raise him as she imagined. So her motherly hood instincts kicked in shooting it out. Even with Detective Wilson gone, his partner lives and seeks justice to be served to the fullest.

Little Ki Ki was given a one million dollar cash bond. Money she has with all of her investments in crypto currency, Dodge, Bit Coin, Real Estate and other business investments her and Karin has. The only problem, Little Ki Ki has been unable to connect with Karin since she was release on bail, close to three months ago. This put Little Ki Ki on edge, thinking about the one she loves, being out there alone to tend to all of their money and properties. Little Ki Ki is hoping the MS-13 goons didn't get to her. She called her cell phone number and house number every day, since she found out how much her bail is. Full of excitement knowing she would be out holding the hommies down, doing what she could for them. Now she can't even get out, depending on Karin who is not answering the phone. Little Ki Ki was trying to locate her fast, before they shipped her out to another federal holding facility. They have been to Texas federal facility, Nevada holding facility, then Clinton County Correctional Federal holding facility, before sending them to Illinois. Word traveled fast throughout the federal holding facility of Little Ki Ki's presence. Especially with the impact she had on the Chicago and the Midwest, with her lady goon style of business, backed with undercutting the Mendez twins, who are cartel connected. Little Ki Ki without question has a lot of love from Chicago's Gangsta Disciples, and Vice Lords. The females were held on the top floor of the ten story facility. The males on the first five floors. The mess hall, schools, and gym areas on the floors in between. The Mendez twins also catching wind, that Little Ki Ki is here at the Illinois Federal holding facility. The Mendez twins are also a part of the reason, Little Ki Ki and the team is in jail. They had one of their street soldiers volunteer her identity and distribution business's to the FBI. This made them surveil her twenty four hours a day. Even getting closer than they preferred, gathering Intel.

"What it do folk?" Little Ki Ki asked this Latina with short black hair, a dark butch stare, pudgy face, thick body, her ears having gages in them. The butch Latina didn't respond, only staring at Little Ki Ki, placing her on high alert. She isn't about to let this bitch get he drop on her.

Little Ki Ki looked around the day room area, making sure she wasn't being closed in on. Also to be aware of her surroundings, in this concrete jungle of wild bitches trying to make a name for themselves. The other women are playing card and board games. Some on the phones, the others on the kiosk sending out emails or ordering commissary. Suga Baby and Red Rain are also with Little Ki Ki on the same block, sitting in the day room area. Each of them in their tan jump suits, no makeup, just their natural beauty.

"That bitch make a move, we going to show her how it's done, dragging her all over this mutha fucka". Red Rain said to Little Ki Ki, also picking up on the butch looking Latina's unwanted stares. "Watch that other bitch too". She added, seeing another Latina coming out her cell leaning over the second tier, looking down, before nodding her head to the thick butch Latina.

Right then, she came off of the wall fast, moving towards Little Ki Ki, who is seeming to be watching TV until she caught the fast movement. Immediate, Little Ki Ki spotted the shank in this bitch's right hand. Red Rain and Suga Baby, moved just as fast, going around the table, closing in on this thick Latina. Little Ki Ki took the pen that was on the table being used to keep score for the Spades game. "Es para La Mendez hermanos!" She said, thrusting the shank forward, thinking she caught Little Ki Ki slipping. Little Ki Ki moved quick, side stepping the shank only to slam the pen into the Latina's thick cheek. At the same time, Suga Baby and Red Rain taking the chairs hitting the Latina over the head with them, dropping her. The block officer seeing this abrupt commotion, hit the all guards button, sounding the alarm and flashing lights. It didn't stop them from stomping the Latina, making her pay for disrespecting their gangsta.

Little Ki Ki picked up the shank the Latina dropped, preparing to stab her until her arm got tired, at the same time a dozen CERT team officers came in fast with tasers, shotguns armed with rubber bullets. All inmates not involved, knew to hit the floor fast or they will be shot, just as Little Ki Ki, Red Rain and Suga Baby, got hit with rubber bullets and tasers. Little Ki Ki's body thrusting back dropping the shank. They closed in on her fast, taking aim, securing the cuffs on her. Suga Baby and Red Rain, was also hit with the taser excessively. Their screams filling the day room area.

"You better be glad they shot me. You fucked with the wrong gangsta, trying to come at me!" Little Ki Ki said staring intently at the downed Latina, with the snapped off pen, still wedged in her face. Little Ki Ki even locked eyes with the Latina on the second tier remembering her face at the same time, wishing she could have gotten to her, for giving the green light. "Stop tasing them you bitch ass fake police!" Little Ki Ki snapped, seeing the officers pressing the taser into their flesh.

"Shut the fuck up before we slam you to the floor, tasing you!" The CERT officer stated aggressively removing each of them from the block, taking them to the Restricted Housing Unit. The Latina went to medical, before she too was sent to the hole. Now with this attack, they all have to remain on high alert. Especially with the first Latina failing, more will come by any means necessary.

Chapter 2

Down in Virginia, the FBI put TK in F.C.I-GILMORE, a federal prison. They pulled strings in doing this, to further shake TK up while giving him a glimpse of how the rest of his life is going to be spent behind the walls and fences of federal prison. The FBI is also fucking with TK moving him more frequent than the women. This attempt to keep him stressed, unsettled, on edge it didn't work. It's all jail shit to him, so changing the scenery is a plus, breaking his days up. This shuffle did make it hard for him to obtain and keep legal counsel apprised to his whereabouts. This is also a part of the FBI's strategy, not giving him adequate time to prepare. The FBI knew they could push this tactic to its legal limits, not wanting to blow this case they worked hard to put together against this organization.

Within a few days of being at F. C. I.-Gilmore, TK heard his name come over the intercom.

"Inmate King, report to the officer's desk". His cell door buzzed, allowing him to exit. At the same time, he's wondering what it's for. He walked up on the guards at the desk outside of the control bubble, where the guards secured everything, controlling all doors, while watching all of the cameras on the block and yard.

"You have a legal visit". The guard said, handing TK a signed pass to the visiting room area. "Soon as the control buzz you out, go down the walk way to the building at the end of the walk way. They'll see you buzzing you into that area for a visit". The guard said.

TK followed the instructions given, still trying to figure out who came to see him, since his many attempts to secure counsel failed. He entered he building following the signs to the visiting room, where he was stripped out, put into a visiting jump suit with white canvas slip shoes.

"Your visit is in the second room on the left when you step out". The guard said. Soon as he entered the room he noticed two well groomed dressed men. One looking to be Italian, wearing a navy blue tailored Tom Ford suit, with a imported silk tie, Tom Ford shoes, a fifty thousand dollar rose gold Rolex Yacht Master with a blue dial. Tanned skin from expensive Caribbean vacations on a private yacht. He's also clean shaven, white teeth, adding to his wealthy look of power, blue eyes dark brown hair combed back. Only forty five years old, yet a powerhouse in the legal and many businesses he's connected to.

"Mr. King, you're a hard man to keep track of with all this shuffling around the feds are doing with you". The Italian looking lawyer said extending his hand, shaking TK's hand, as he continued to speak. " I'm Salvator Aielo, I have offices in New York, Miami and California. Anyway take a seat over there, so we can get down to business". TK glanced over at the other well groomed man off to the side yet behind Salvator. Salvator failing to introduce him, which kept TK alert to see what his position is. He at first glance looked to be white, but he's not, TK figured. He is looking serious not saying a word, only observing. "Like I said let's get down to it. With what they have against you, they can and will throw the book at you if you take this to trial and lose". Salvator said being blunt, to see what direction his client want to go.

"I'm not worried about me doing time. I just want the women to be set free. I'll take all the weight of the federal government has to offer me". TK responded. Salvator glanced over his shoulder at his associate, before addressing TK.

"That's honorable and all with this street code thing you're upholding, but that's not how the federal government works. You plea out to forty years and with good time, good health and hope, you can be home in thirty or less, after I file a sentence reconsideration". Salvator said flipping through his papers, looking at what the feds charges are against TK. "I seen guys get that for a few kilos, and from the looks of this they have you moving tons of cocaine up and down the east coast".

"How the fuck they even tag me and my team? We don't move stupid or flashy". TK questioned, knowing he ran a tight operation.

"You pissed someone off. Not you directly, but someone close to you because they have informants alleging your lady friend was invading on territory ran by the Mendez twins". Salvator responded, having his resources to get this Intel that's not exactly in the paperwork.

"So these mutha fuckas ratted, setting the trap that brought the heat on us?" TK asked, becoming angered by the thought, wanting to personally down them bitch ass twins Salvator just mentioned. TK unaware of the beef Little Ki Ki had with the twins that lead to this.

"Mr. King, with Rosanna Santiago gone, the weight is yours to carry. Now me being the best lawyer in this business. I took the initiative to make the government a proposal on your behalf, in exchange for no jail time". "For who? I know you ain't talking about me, like I'm a fold? Who the fuck I'm a fold on, my girls and the little hommie Ki Ki?" He asked aggressively, being offended by the gesture of turning on his team or anyone to become a rat.

"Calm down Mr. King, I'm here to do a job. As your attorney, your freedom is most important thing to me. So listen, and listen to me carefully". Salvator said, adjusting his position in his seat, looking on at TK.

"They want Hector Sanchez. You're the only one that is in line, that he would trust to send you tons of cocaine into America. You do this, helping the federal government take him down, and you'll be set free today along with your lady friends. Just sign right here and by the time you get back to the block, they'll be calling your name for you to pack your shit to leave ". Salvator said trying to sell the idea of being a rat to TK.

"For real? All I have to do is sign this paper and I'm out?" TK said mocking Salvator, taking the paper as he stood from the chair, he started tearing the paper up, shredding it into pieces.

"You got to be a stupid mutha fucka to think I'm a flip on the same people that showed me love, putting me in the position of power. Like I said before, I wanted the crown, so I'm going to where this shit to the grave". TK

16

stated firmly, being a true G honoring the code of the streets.

"And rightfully so, you deserve to wear this crown hermano". The other well groomed man said, finally speaking, allowing his Latino accent to be heard. Salvator started smiling as he leaned back in his chair looking at TK, respecting him and his firm position of being loyal to the code of silence. TK picked up quick on what just took place, seeing he'd just been tested. No test needed, his gangsta or street honor wouldn't let him be anything else but true to this shit he lives and will die for. Even if he has never met Hector, he would never turn on the connect.

"Now that you finally decided to speak, who are you?" TK asked.

"I'm Armando Osario. I'm Hector's right hand man, his sicario if needed". Armando responded. Armando standing six foot even, slim built with his Spanish accent permeating in his speech. He has a full beard cut close, shaped up with razor precision, flowing up to his close cut on the sides, feathered on top. Thick yet groomed eyebrows. Armando is wearing a black Armani tailored suit, with a blood red shirt with a matching tie. He's also boasting a Gold Daytona Rolex worth ninety five thousand, having the blood red dial. Armando spoke with calm, yet each word delivered with the presence of his position of power. "In this business, having insurance is vital". Armando said.

"Yeah, I heard that from someone before". TK responded, referring to when La Reina said that to him at her condo, before she was murdered on his rise to power.

17

Her insurance became the bloody massacre of his and Suga Baby's family, backed by the other bull shit that came with Don Rico and the Latin Kings wanting revenge.

"Lucky for you hermano, La Viejas spoke highly of you, even considering you and your team as familia. We in Mexico value our family, so we never abandon or leave them behind. This situation you're in will dissipate with a few phone calls. Besides you didn't physically get caught with or touch anything. All they have is hearsay from CIs, we'll leave that side of things for you to handle ". Armando said.

TK took a few seconds to process what he's hearing. This situation as real as it is, doesn't feel right. Even if he comes out from under this fed beef, how would this shit look or even make him feel? Besides how the fuck they going to make that shit happen? TK's thinking, knowing the feds don't usually make arrest they don't have evidence to back it up.

"Your lady friends, Keisha and Shandrea have detainers from Pennsylvania, for homicide and attempted homicide. So for right now, nothing can be done for them. Now Takia, we can bail her out using our company resources". Armando said, referring to Little Ki Ki. It's also the first time TK heard her real name being used. "Nothing in this life is free. I know in return you and Hector want something?" TK stated.

"You already gave us your loyalty. You've also made us a lot of money. We want to keep this moving forward". "Being released from federal custody to do exactly what they suspected I was doing, isn't the smartest move". TK responded.

"It's the only move, the moment we redeem and honor La Vieja's insurance on you and your team". Armando stated with a calm serious tone, then added. " Or you and your team can live your life behind these prison walls reflecting on a life you once had far away from your son, who will end up in foster care, because you don't have family to look after him". For the first time, the gangsta shield TK kept up was penetrated by the reality of indirectly abandoning his son, leaving him with no parents. TK's gritting his teeth thinking about his son. He now knows he has to get to as soon as possible.

"Okay, just do what is needed to get me to my son. I'll do what I have to for you and Hector. I want insurance for the women when the time comes, you'll make it possible for my son's mother to be in his life with us". TK stated thinking smart, knowing he's in a position now to request insurance he knows they'll honor, with him being their affiliate. TK also knowing that the cartel has their connections to make moves. What he doesn't know, is how deeply rooted and globally connected Salvator is, being a go to guy for a lot of people, which puts him in a position to be the guy that knows a guy to get things done always and at any time.

"Like I said hermano, familia is everything. We don't leave anyone behind. When the time is right Salvator will see to it, that it gets handled". Armando said extending his hand, shaking TK's hand sealing their agreement. Salvator also stood, shaking TK's hand.

19

"We'll see you in a few days down in Mexico. Someone will be here to take you to the airport, using a private jet from Hector's fleet". Salvator said. TK's demeanor shifting seeing the light shining on this dark situation he found himself in. Life in prison is what he would have been facing with the amount of years he would have gotten. Now because of his loyalty, honor and respect towards La Vieja, it has went a long way, setting him free from his confines. Even after her graphic murder, she had his best interest to look after him and his team. She definitely was a true boss bitch, thinking ahead, securing her legacy. Her family will benefit off of the money TK generates, sending back to Mexico to Hector. All due to her loyalty, along with being bread winner for the powerful cartel boss, who now has control over the majority of the cocaine flowing through Mexico into the United States, giving him absolute power.

Chapter 3

Two days later in Illinois over at the federal holding facility. Little Ki Ki's name was being called over the intercom of the Restricted Housing Unit, followed by two officers coming to her cell door. Suga Baby and Red Rain also hearing them call Little Ki Ki, so they are standing on their door looking out to see what's going on. "Bucannon pack your shit, your bail was posted". The officer said.

Little Ki Ki hearing this, became excited thinking Karin found her finally, posting the one million dollar bond. The cartel using their American business, having one of their associates post her bond. The guards escorting Little Ki Ki are also members of the CERT team that roughed her and the others up. She stared them down as she exited the cell, never forgetting their faces.

"We love you Ki Ki!" Suga Baby yelled out, then added. "Please find my son and look after him". Little Ki Ki always being hard, was moved by her motherly emotional plea to find her son that was ripped from her grasp the day of her arrest. Also hearing the pain and strain in her voice, it alone spoke volumes.

"You already know I got you baby girl. I'm a hold y'all down. We family ya feel me. As for junior, soon as I get him, I'm a send you some flicks ya hear me? Aye now be safe around here. I got a lot of love for y'all boss bitches". Little Ki Ki said as she exited the block, making her way out to the front gate, where she was given the clothes she was arrested in. When she walk through the front gate of the prison, a Lincoln Town car awaited her with a driver. She looked around wondering where Karin is, still thinking that she's the one that posted her bail. If she was she should be here greeting me. Little Ki Ki is thinking. Nothing. No Karin, just the driver. "Where would you like me to take you Ms. Bucannon?" The driver asked with his Ukrainian accent. He didn't have any other instructions other than to show up at a set time.

"You have a cell phone?" She asked.

"Yes I do".

"Let me see ya phone folk".

The driver passed her the phone. She called up Karin wanting answers to why she couldn't reach her? Why isn't she here to greet her? Why she didn't post her bail? Why she didn't try finding her even with the feds shuffling them around? So many questions, so many thoughts of what has taken place. All in need of answers. The phone rang four times before it picked up.

" Hello ". A child's voice answered.

This threw Little Ki Ki off for a second, making her pull away from the phone looking at the number she just dialed, checking to make sure it's the right one. It's the right number. Now the question is, whose child is answering Karin's phone.

"Who is this?" Little Ki Ki questioned. The young child sounding like she could be four or five years old.

22

"I'm Leah, do you want my mommy?" The little girl said full of excitement.

Having heard this is shocking Little Ki Ki's emotional senses. As far as she knows, Karin didn't have any kids. If she did, how could she keep a secret like this from the one woman she claim to love? More important, why? " Where ya mommy at now Leah?" Little Ki Ki asked. Truthfully hoping somehow someway this little girl answered Karin's phone happens to be a family member of Karin's.

"Um, in the kitchen with my daddy". The little girl responded as she hurried towards the kitchen with the phone in hand. " Mommy! Mommy the phone! Somebody want you mom!" The little girl innocently yelled out. The reality of betrayal from Karin is making Little Ki Ki feel pain, especially if she has a man and a child, that she didn't know about. This would also fully explain why she didn't bail her out or why she wasn't seeking to find out where she was in the federal system. Even why she couldn't reach her the many times she called. Little Ki Ki became silent, angered and emotional as she listened in to the other side of the call.

"Didn't I tell you to leave the phone alone". Karin said to Leah, her ever so familiar voice.

Little Ki Ki recognized immediately, acknowledging the little girl calling out to her as mommy. Karin snatched the phone from her daughter looking at the incoming number that's anonymous, however only one person has this number. She had no way of accessing a million dollars cash for bond, Karin is thinking. Especially with her having financial control over everything. Karin placed the phone to her ear, quietly listening in, awaiting her to speak, at the same time wanting to know how much her daughter said over the phone as well as if she heard her speaking with her husband Daren Rucker. The silence between them lasted for a minute before Karin's husband spoke, seeing she's frozen in silence.

"Who is it honey?"

Hearing this ignited a flame inside of Little Ki Ki forcing her to hang up the phone, wanting to come face to face with Karin. To look into her eyes seeing why she lied, deceiving her all of this time. Karin's deep cover lesbian role, tricking Little Ki Ki into falling in love, trusting her, making her vulnerable which allowed her to do as she wished. It is without question the greatest con, even more, the greatest illusion of lies and seduction to get the reward of riches. Little Ki Ki is thinking not knowing who she fell for or who Karin really is now with this discovery of her having a whole family, husband and child. She handed the driver his phone back having her mind made up on what is needed to be done to get to the bottom of this, in order to get all the money Karin has of hers since she doesn't deserve a dime of it for her deceit.

"Take me to Harrisburg, Pennsylvania, I have business there that needs my immediate attention".

"Yes Ms. Bucannon. Oh before I forget, this is for you ma'am". The driver said, handing her a envelope with twenty grand in one hundred dollar bills, with a phone number on the outside of the envelope. She didn't feel like calling the number right now, especially the space her heart and mind is in right now. Only thing she can think of is getting answers to her questions along with securing

24

her millions she entrusted Karin with thinking that this woman loved her as much as she did her. As the driver drove off towards Pennsylvania, Little Ki Ki closed her eyes with her head back, trying to process all that is going on. How she started from the hood, getting money, saving every dollar, having a vision to get out of the hood. Even when she crossed paths with Karin, no signs of deceit, only affection good sex and her sharing the same visions of real estate and investing to have a out of the game. Little Ki Ki is wanting to know if she does have a husband and child, how could she live two lives without either of them being suspicious? Is her husband in on the con or is she just that good in misleading all in her scheme to get money by any means necessary? This bitch is diabolical for that shit. Ki Ki is thinking and feeling, in between opening her eyes staring out of the window, wanting to come face to face with the woman she fell in love with, willing to give her the world, instead this bitch stole it, placing a target on her and all she really love and care about. Little Ki Ki's thoughts tormenting her as she's reflecting back on it all, even the phone call she just had changing her perception of love and life, at the same time leaving a burning scar deep in her heart. Now she's trying to figure out how she's going to make Karin pay for her betrayal. So many thoughts of what is going to be next, each vision ending with blood being spilled, especially with millions on the line, coupled with a broken heart, lies and betrayal that can't be undone or forgiven.

Chapter 4

When the driver finally made it to Little Ki Ki's house in Pennsylvania, the first thing she noticed is a Remax Reality Group real estate sign, with the bold red letters that read SOLD. Another razor sharp blow, burning deep in her heart as she exited the car walking up on the door, ringing the bell, knocking in disbelief that this could be happening to her.

"This bitch got me fucked up, turning her back on me". Little Ki Ki said aloud angered by what's unfolding, realizing she's been financially and emotionally conned. Little Ki Ki turned to head back to the car when she noticed the neighbor standing on her porch preparing to leave. She made her way over to the house, wanting to see if they have any information on Karin. "How you doing?" Little Ki Ki said to the mid forty Italian-American woman with brown hair, tanned skin, makeup on point, wearing the latest fashions, all thanks to her husband who's a brain surgeon.

"Hey Takia, where ya been at? I see ya sold the house". The neighbor asked.

"I was on a government funded vacation. Karin sold the house while I was gone". Little Ki Ki responded, pissed to think she's been betrayed by the one she truly loves.

"You know I asked her where you were, especially when I seen her with handsome young fella, that came around. She was always shifting subjects to business, telling me I can get well over we paid for this house, even triple if we act now. She gave me her new business card". The neighbor said.

Little Ki Ki was thinking this bitch was probably trying to con the neighbors, with convincing them they could sell for triple. A con artist doesn't make a move like that, unless they can benefit from it.

"Did she say where she's moving to?"

"This fancy new development in Hershey, Pennsylvania".

"Mrs. Giacanna, can I take a look at that business card she gave you. I loss contact with her, as you can see go away for a few months and things suddenly change".

"One second, let me run into the house to get it for ya".

Mrs. Giacanna said turning to head back into the house, wanting to help Little Ki Ki since she viewed her as a good neighbor. Little Ki Ki turned to her driver holding up her index finger signifying she wanted him to wait a minute. He pulled the car up to the neighbor's house where Little Ki Ki standing. Within a few minutes Mrs. Giacanna popped back out of the house with the business card given to her by Karin.

"Here ya go Takia, I hope you two reconnect so you can be happy like I've always seen the two of ya". Mrs. Giacanna said handing her the card. Little Ki Ki looking

28

on at the card, knowing when she does reconnect with Karin, it won't be for smiles and love. Only her money, blood and pain, to make her feel appeased for this level of betrayal. Little Ki Ki memorized the info on the card before handing it back to Mrs. Giacanna.

"I really appreciate Mrs. Giacanna".

"It's no problem, I want to help you two lovebirds, so we can have our ladies night at your place. I really enjoyed those times". Mrs. Giacanna said, not realizing those times are long gone, all because of Karin's betrayal. Little Ki Ki gave off a empty smile, before turning walking away to the car, with her mind racing with thoughts of what she wants to do, when she comes face to face with Karin.

Once inside of the car she exhaled a stressed yet anxious breath.

"Yo we have a long day ahead of us, so if you hungry or have to use the bathroom, let's get it done now. Then we going to get me a phone, some clothes and a hotel so I can get fresh, then we going to track my millions down".

Little Ki Ki feeling a step closer to getting shit done, with having a direction to go in finding Karin. The driver hearing the part about her millions, is now tuned in. He's along for the ride, knowing he will be rewarded for his services. The driver followed her instructions, taking her shopping, securing a phone. They also drove into the hoods of Harrisburg, allowing her to scope out the city she love and respect, especially the YG niggas that always held her down, moving product and riding out with her when needed. She plans on linking back up with them, once she got back in position to even have a conversation with them. Right now she feels like her absence let them

29

down with the supply. She also noticed this when she drove through the South Acres, seeing all the Spanish mutha fuckas trapping. They're set up just as they were before, meaning they have the product to supply the hood and its demand for it, which gives them the power and position. Product supplied by the Mendez twins, after they ratted out Little Ki Ki indirectly having one of their soldiers give the FBI information, that lead to the investigation. Information Little Ki Ki is still unaware of. However when the time does come, when she discovers that it was the twins she ran out of Chicago, that was the reason behind her downfall, she'll make them pay in blood, with a graphic demise. The Mendez twins, unaware of Little Ki Ki's release.

"Ivan take me to Hershey so I can handle this business". Little Ki Ki said to her Ukrainian driver, after they went to the hood securing a black steel 32. automatic, from the P-Funk projects. The little hommies down there already knowing who she is, so they didn't hesitate to bless her. Even if it's not the gun she really wanted, it has bullets and a extra clip, plus it'll get the job done along with getting her point across if need be. The young bucks from the hood was also looking for her to come back to bless them with those numbers she once promised them, especially with the high prices and low grade product they're getting now. The first stop is to the address that was on the business card, a real estate company Karin started called Diamond Real Estate. With Karin's name listed as the CEO. The driver pulled up to the well to do real estate company, having a white Porsche

Truck along with a candy apple red Bentley truck, sitting out in front.

Each of the trucks present, adding to the affluent lifestyle of those who could afford to live in Hershey and its sumptuous developments.

"Ms. Bucannon do you need me to come inside with you?" Ivan Swortkoski her driver asked.

"Say man, I'm no Miss, call me Little Ki Ki or just Ki Ki ya feel me? Nah I'm good on my end, just wait for me, ya hear me?"

"Yeah I hear you Ki Ki". Ivan responded in his deep rooted Ukrainian accent.

Ivan has been working hard since he arrived in America a few years ago. Even sending money back to his home country, until the war broke out with Russian invading Ukraine. Now with just his wife Elenora and their seven year old son here with him in America. Elenora understood her husband's long days working, knowing it provides for them and family back in Ukraine. Ivan isn't no stranger to violence, coming from where he was raised. Little Ki Ki entered the fancy real estate establishment, wearing her black Nike sweat suit, with a black Yankees baseball cap. Soon as she walked in, the two employees a male and female standing behind the counter seem to turn their nose up at her like she doesn't belong here inside of this prestigious area or real estate company.

"I'm sorry, are you lost?" The blond haired, grey eyed female with a vacuous smile asked as if she is truly concerned, having her hand on the phone ready to speed dial 911, seeing this thugged out looking female coming her way.

31

"Do it look like I'm lost bitch?!" Little Ki Ki verbally fired back, coming up to the counter. The male looking on at Ki Ki wondering if he should answer her, especially with the hard look she's giving him. "Where's Karin?"

"I'm sorry, she only takes scheduled appointments. No walk ins". The blond responded, only angering Little Ki Ki with that snobby ass smirk on her face.

"Oh appointments only huh?" Little Ki Ki mocked, before removing the .32 automatic aiming it at the blond, before adding. "Schedule me in for one right now".

"Oh God! Please don't shoot me. She's not even here right now". The blond responded in fear, seeing death coming her way fast.

"You think I'm stupid? Don't fucking lie to me! I see them trucks out in front". Little Ki Ki said slipping her finger inside of the trigger guard, ready to send slugs in this snobby bitch's face.

"They're her trucks under the company's name. She leaves them there to look more appealing and prestigious to customers". The blond responded hoping this answer is suffice enough to not be shot. Little Ki Ki couldn't just leave without finding her, where she lives or how to track her down.

"When is she expected back here?"

"She called in first thing this morning cancelling her appoints or diverting them to other agents, to show properties off". The male responded.

"I need her home address. Anything less your shift ends right here and now". Little Ki Ki said, meaning every word. The blond racing her fingers across the computer's keyboard accessing the address.

32

"Milton Hershey Estates, 727 White Deer Road". The blond blurted out, wanting Little Ki Ki to be gone.

"Y'all call the cops or warn this bitch, I'll come back for ya shawty and put bullets all in ya face and body". Little Ki Ki threatened, before exiting with speed, focusing on tracking Karin down to secure her millions while getting revenge. Soon as she closed the car door, she relayed the address to Ivan. "Seven two seven, White Deer Road, in the Milton Hershey Estates". He punched the info into his navigational system before heading to their destination. Little Ki Ki having so many thoughts of securing her physical cash money along with her crypto currency and properties.

Within minutes they arrived to the upscale community boasting homes ten thousand square feet and up, with all of the lavish amenities. Ivan pulled up to the address he was given, seeing that the home has a four car garage with foreign cars parked in it, all over a hundred thousand. Inside of this large home is has two living rooms, home theater, fully stock sports bar on the lower level, two fire places one in the formal living room, the other in the master bedroom suite, The master bedroom balcony overlooking the large yard with a pool. Five large bedrooms, a gym, large swimming pool out back with a gazebo, pool house, outdoor grill and kitchen for entertaining guest. Little Ki Ki exited the car making her way into the home through the open garage door, where the yellow Ferrari 450 is parked along side the Bugatti, Aston Martin DB9 and CSL65 AMG Mercedes Benz.

"This bitch is having her way with my money". Little Ki Ki said in a low tone as she passed the cars, making her way inside of the house. Once inside she removed the .32 automatic, safety off one in the chamber ready to get it popping. She closed in on the voices she can hear, leading her to the leisure living room off the kitchen area. The little girl she spotted, looking to be five years old, having black hair, green eyes, a biracial Asian-American with Daren her father being a white male.

Leah spotted Little Ki Ki entering the room, so she started pointing towards her.

"Look daddy". Leah said innocently.

Daren is sitting on the couch watching TV when he turned only to be greeted with a gun staring back at him. "We have money in the safe, just don't hurt my daughter". He expressed in great fear for their lives, unaware of who this person is standing before him.

"Where is she?" Ki Ki questioned ready to get to it.

"Who?" He responded dumbfounded.

"Karin, where is she?" Little Ki Ki now closing in on Leah taking hold of her hand, so the perspective and level of seriousness fully sets in. His eyes widen at the sight of her taking Leah's hand, becoming a threat to her.

"She's in the shower".

"Let's go up to wait on her to finish". Little Ki Ki said directing him to lead the way up to the master bedroom. When they entered the room, they could see Karin was freshly out of the shower.

Her hair still wet, as she's getting dressed.

"Mommy look". Leah blurted out, not realizing this person holding her hand is her mother's ex lover, as well as the person who wants to bring harm to her for the level of betrayal and deception she imposed. Karin turned to

34

her daughter's voice, only to see Little Ki Ki standing there with a gun aimed at her husband. She froze in shock and fear, never thinking her con would lead to this threat to her husband and child. Little Ki Ki, also having conflicting thoughts and emotions, not knowing how she would act once she set eyes on this woman she gave her all to, mentally, physically and emotionally. The other side of her, being the thugged out Atlanta G, she wanted to make this bitch pay in blood for testing her gangsta.

"This is not like the love I have for you or the relationship we have Takia". Karin said wanting to take control of this unwieldy situation, that came at her unexpectedly.

"Yeah, this don't feel or look like love to me. You can have this family shit. All I want is my money nothing less". Little Ki Ki said staring intently at Karin. Karin having seen that look in her eyes before, so she has to think fast. "I have two million cash that you left at the house. The other money as you know is invested and tied up". Karin said trying to pacify Little Ki Ki with a small portion of the close to fifteen million she tried to run away with.

"I loved you enough to give you the world Karin. Now with your betrayal, I hate you enough to kill all you love, to make you feel a fraction of the anger and pain inside of me. So if you try to play me with a little bit of paper, when I have well over ten million. I will leave your husband where he stands". Ki Ki vented, shoving the pistol to the side of Daren's head, sending a jolting fear through him and Karin.

"Noooo! I'll give you the crypto currency account numbers, to do as you please with it. It's where the bulk of your money is anyway". Karin pleaded as she writing down the account numbers. She came over trying to hand it to Little Ki Ki. "Sit it on the bed". She did just that, wanting to appease her . Little Ki Ki didn't even want to know why or how she chose her to con, she only wanted back what was hers. As for Karin, she never expected to fall hard in love as she did. When Ki Ki went to jail, it gave her the perfect out, or so she thought. Even Karin's husband was out of the loop, only thinking she was always travelling for work, meaning the government, at least that's what she told him, staying busy making money, sending it back to him in between finding ways back to their home, when Ki Ki wasn't around due to her street life. Karin was always in control of the con until now.

"If I punch these numbers in on your computer right now, it will give me access to my crypto?" Little Ki Ki asked, staring intently at Karin, checking to see if she's still trying to con her way out. Little Ki Ki took hold of the paper. "Come over here". She directed Daren over to the lap top on the night stand. "Punch these numbers in. They better be the right numbers, your life depends on it". She added before looking at Karin, who is standing firm, seeming sure.

Daren nervously ran his fingers across the keyboard entering the numbers given. A beeping sound filled the air, signifying the wrong code was entered. Karin knows if the wrong code is entered multiple times the account will lockout, no one gets the money. Karin also hearing the computer beeping, so she tried to explain. "I'm nervous, I must have written the wrong number down".

36

Karin said. Little Ki Ki looked at her then squeezed the trigger blowing Daren's brains out the other side of his skull, spraying the white curtains. Karin screamed, jumping back shocked by this abrupt murder of her husband. Her con has gone too far, costing the life of her child's father.

"Daddy noooo!". Leah cried seeing him slumped over. Little Ki Ki clearly focused on revenge and getting her money.

"Your daughter is next, if you want to keep playing these mutha fucking games, like you don't know how I get down for my money ".

"I'm sorry babe".

"Don't fucking babe me you conning ass bitch!" Little Ki Ki snapped aiming the gun at Karin. She put her hands up blocking her face as if she could stop a bullet.

"I'm sorry, here's the right numbers, just don't hurt my daughter, I don't care what you do to me, she's innocent". Karin pleaded to deaf ears. Her con brought all of this on her and the family she loves.

"I want the code to that safe you have too". Little Ki Ki added, wanting it all. Karin did as she was instructed. Little Ki Ki took pillow cases filling them up with vacuum sealed bags of money, emptying the entire safe. "Can you leave us a little something?" Karin begged as if she's not the greatest con artist that could easily get money by scheming someone else, or through the new real estate business.

"You won't be needing it". Little Ki Ki responded pointing the gun to Karin's heart firing off two rounds, wanting to destroy her heart just as she's done to hers.

37

Then in the same swift motion she turned the gun on Leah firing a round into her screaming mouth, before exiting the house with the bags of money, leaving behind a bloody murder scene.

Little Ki Ki is now in this cold hearted state of mind, tuned back in to getting this money, bodying anyone in her way.

"Take me back to my hotel, after that you can go. I appreciate your services. I got it from here". She said passing Ivan a couple stacks of money, totaling a hundred grand. Ivan looked at the amount of money knowing it would go a long way in helping his family here and back in Ukraine. As for Little Ki Ki she bought his silence, so she could focus back on the takeover she left behind, minus the love she wanted so bad with Karin. This alone is going to make her numb to emotions while being a stone cold gangsta bitch.

Chapter 5

Sinaloa, Mexico the next day. The private G5 jet with custom amenities fit for a king, is landing on the secured private airstrip, owned by Hector Sanchez. One of Mexico's notorious cartel figures, known for his bloody wrath and endless body count in his rise to power. TK is on the private jet with Salvator and Armando who were also present when he exited the federal prison, free of all charges, thanks to their endless deep rooted connections, making this all possible. Hector personally wanted to meet with TK, an American goon, La Vieja spoke highly of, vouching for him and his team. He also wanted to put a face physically to the person he's about to trust with tons of his product. Hector held La Vieja with high respect, especially how she brought the Mexican cartel way of life into America, not taking any bullshit, killing off rivals and rats. He also was told about TK being loyal to the code of silence even if he'd never met the cartel boss, he didn't break or bend becoming a snitch.

"We're here amigo". Armando said seeing TK looking out of the window, wondering why they didn't land at a regular airport. That regular lifestyle is way behind him the moment he took on this task of replacing La Vieja. It all started coming into view as he continued to look on at the four hundred acres of land, a private hangar for the jets, armed Mexican goons on Hector's payroll. All with fully automatic rifles ranging from AK-47s to M-16s, securing the compound. They exited the private jets once it halted inside of the hangar. There a they got into one of the three Land Rovers taking them to the main house, that's a twenty five thousand square foot mansion protected around the clock. The large mansion having two guest houses on each side of the pool house. No need for a traditional garage, he has a hangar style garage for his twenty plus exotic custom cars, even limited edition cars. Every where Hector goes there is a convoy of security protecting him.

The Land Rovers stopped in front of the large circular driveway, greeted by more security.

"Armando, Salvator, who do we have here?" The lead home security goon questioned, double checking to see who he is.

"Tracy 'TK' King, a very close associate of La Vieja's and now a good friend of ours, here to meet with Hector as he requested". Armando responded, watching the security guards pat TK down along with Salvator. They didn't touch Armando, knowing he's Hector's right hand man that would give his life for him. TK now seeing first hand, the next level of power this coke game offers being a cartel boss with hundreds of Mexican goons armed protecting his compound, as well as his home inside and out. They entered the sumptuous mansion with a thirty foot ceiling in the foyer, white marble floors, crystal imported chandelier, a dual staircase with a elevator in the middle that goes from the second floor to the custom designed lower level with, gym, theater, club, spa and game room.

Soon as they entered the mansion, Hector exited his bedroom smoking a cigar.

"Oye hermano, welcome to mi casa. Es solo para la familia. And from what Rosanna told me and Armando, you are family". Hector said puffing on his cigar blowing cloud of smoke out as he descended down the staircase with gold features. His Mexican security goons standing outside of his room also accompanied him down the steps.

Hector standing five foot five, with a giant's attitude and power. Thick eyebrows, matching his thick mustache. The rest of his face clean shaven. Hector looking thick, weighing two hundred and twenty pounds, nice biceps from lifting, yet still has a gut from eating good Mexican food and drinking beers. It didn't stop him from dressing like a boss with the white silk button up Versace shirt he has open at the top showing off his gold chains encrusted with diamonds, especially the Virgin Mary chain with blue diamonds in her eyes. The tan Polo pants flowing down to his Polo shoes.

"You know who I am hermano, I know who you are. Now let's get to the business side of things. Come follow me". Hector said already having his chef and maids set up the food out by the pool side area. TK, Salvator and Armando all following the boss. He was taking in the large scale of the mansion as well as the level of security to protect it, making it home and very comfortable for the violent cartel boss. What TK isn't taking into perspective about Hector's position of power, being the number one cocaine distributor in the world. The government when they discover who he is, will come for him, his associates to avoid him being replaced and all he has, crippling him from every aspect. In the mean time Hector's only worry is rising cartels wanting what he has, absolute power. This alone keeps Hector on high alert at all times, limiting his trust and associates. Hector's reach is deep rooted, having made friends in powerful places around the world, protecting his best asset, which is himself. They made their way to the back side of the mansion, by the pool side where exotic Mexicanas in and around the pool. TK taking in the these model looking females, appreciating the art of their beauty. Each of the women are here for Hector's choosing, making him in TK's eyes even more of a boss. "Take a seat gentlemen, I have the best food coming out, along with whatever you want to drink". Hector said. His staff came out with the food and drinks as they continued to talk distribution business. "Hermano, I don't know how much Salvator or Armando made you aware of. Everything will be the same as it was for La Vieja. You'll use her avenues at the ports. Sal and Armando will give you more instruction and details. The price she was given will also be yours. Only thing I see different is the increase in shipment, since I have a hundred tons backed up with her absence ". Hector said as he's cutting his steak. He glanced over at TK when he mentioned the quantity.

TK was drinking his tequila, processing what he just heard, knowing a hundred tons is way too much for him to handle. Hector started laughing before saying, "Don't worry hermano, the hundred tons isn't just for you. I have product going to South Africa and Europe".

"Hector, I'm down for whatever is needed of me. I appreciate what y'all did, by getting me out of that situation, that could have buried me forever. One thing I ask, I need to get my son from foster care, then if y'all can honor my insurance on my ladies, I would like them to be a part of this new distribution deal, assisting me taking over the country". TK stated wanting to insure his first loves Suga Baby and Red Rain. Hector ate some of his steak processing his thoughts on what has been proposed by TK. He took his beer chasing down his steak before responding.

"Familia is everything hermano. You want them to be a part of this life you live, then Sal will give you the info needed, to make this all possible. It won't be cheap, just as it won't be easy". Hector said taking a gulp of beer. "Nothing in life worth having is cheap or easy". TK responded. They all gave a brief laughter agreeing with TK. "I like you already hermano. I see a bright future of business with you. La Vieja was right about you being business focused". Hector said. At the same time Salvator's cell phone sounded off. He took the call.

"This is Sal speaking over here".

"Say man, ya driver Ivan gave me this number to call. What it do?"

"What it what?" Salvator questioned not being up on the southern twang. "You should have called this number yesterday upon your release. What took you so long?" He asked.

"I had to handle some business, ya feel me?"

43

"What? Hold on I have someone here you should speak to". Salvator said placing the phone on speaker before handing the phone to TK. He looked at the phone wondering who it is. " It's the tough girl". Sal said, with that being his only description of Little Ki Ki.

"Yo what's good with you?" TK said, excited to hear from his little hommie.

"Say man this is crazy, you free too huh?"

"Yeah it's next level right now".

"Shit got crazy for me day one. Karin conned me for my paper. I put a end to that ya feel me. I needed mine". Little Ki Ki said.

"Where you at right now?"

"In PA, but for how long I don't know".

"This ya line?"

"Yeah man".

"Soon as I touch back, I'm a get at you. Stay low and out of the way little hommie ".

"Say no more folk, I'm focused". She said hanging up, already knowing TK is onto something.

"Sal I need that number before I head back to the states". TK said handing Sal his phone back. "That was my little hommie Ki Ki. She's loyal to the core. She would give her life for this shit". TK added.

"It's good to have people like that around you. Anything less could jeopardize all you have built". Hector said sparking up another cigar having finished eating. "One thing about how I run my organization hermano, there are no excuses. Excuses are like bullets awaiting to kill you and your business. We kill our problems hermano, therefore we don't run into excuses of why this

44

money can't be made or product can't be moved". Hector said making it very clear, no one or nothing will stand in his way to maintain his position of power. His stance on this topic of business, has made TK see why La Vieja moved as violent as she did. Hector's words explained why he's connected at all points of entry into the United states and other countries he sends product to. TK also is aware from the news, even those who build tunnels for the cartels don't live to tell about it, or spend the millions they made building them.

"You don't ever have to worry about any excuses or product being moved. We got shit lockdown in the states. I'll lay down anyone in my way". TK said. Hector blew out a cloud of smoke, giving a brief smile.

"Armando, Sal, I like this hermano, he's real and truthful ". Hector said standing from the table, coming over to TK. "Hermano, take a walk with me". Hector said.

TK stood downing the rest of his shot of tequila, before walking with Hector by the pool side with all of the exotic Latinas, smiling at TK wanting to fuck this American, knowing he's a thugged out boss. Hector looking on at them eyeing TK. " You ladies can have your fun with him after we take care of business". Hector said. The ladies turned on by the invite, awaiting them to finish business. As sexy as these women look, TK's mind isn't on fucking these exotic bitches. He's business focus. Something Hector also noticed when speaking to him. "Hermano I like your laser focus, because it tells me, I will never have any problems with you when it comes to my money. Now as for our communications, we use high tech untraceable cell phones by Kryptail. Each month you'll receive a new one for added security protecting what we have. This also prevents any chance law enforcement trying to figure are system out if they even are aware of what we're doing or who we are. Look around hermano, everything I built here is with security in mind, because I want to remain in power. We all want this level of power hermano, but I say to you, don't ever fuck up thinking you can take my power. I'll be trusting you with tons, and in return I'll make you richer than you've ever been. Any problems you have, we kill them off until their blood line no longer exist". Hector said staring at TK making sure he understood every word spoken, along with his new position and role in this organization. TK didn't even respond, only extending his hand giving Hector a firm handshake, looking one another in the eyes with respect, having a mutual understanding of this next level business that's about to take place, changing everything in TK's life.

Chapter 6

Two months passed by, Little Ki Ki is back in full swing of things, getting the love and respect from the Harrisburg YGs, who assisted her in taking the city back over, including the South Acres. The Latin King goons couldn't fuck with the low prices or the quality of the product. Nor could they fuck with the thugged out YG niggas, doing drive bys, walk bys all to clear the hood for her rise to power. Ki Ki even took them out to Chicago with her while she's linking up with King Black, a Gangsta Disciple leader who is moving the product for her out there before the set back.

Today they're meeting up at the tower projects on the top floor, overlooking the hood. King Black is a muscular built nigga, that did hard time for gunning down a rival gang member, over fifteen years ago. Now the forty five year old OG of the streets, is focused on not only running the gang, he's employing them to get as much money as they want as long as they're hungry. King Black a dark skinned nigga standing five foot eleven, wearing a white tank top, no jewels only the twin snub nose .357 magnums he totes on his waist line. One in front the other on his back side, giving him two chances to bang out.

47

"Little Ki Ki out here in the streets got word saying them Spanish niggas lined you up for position". King Black said as he sat two bags of money down for the bricks she just dropped on them. Little Ki Ki wasn't aware the feds got onto her or the team through doing business out this way.

"What Spanish niggas folk?" She asked looking curious.

"Them twins you ran out of here".

"Say word man".

"No lies my nigga". King Black responded.

"They fucked with the wrong G, ya feel me? They got at me and my team behind that bullshit. A rat is a rat, no matter how they eating the cheese, ya hear me. They going pay for that shit".

"Whatever you thinking little hommie, my team will ride with you. Them greedy mutha fuckas keep hitting my phone with them high ass prices and cut work". He said.

Echoes of gunfire can be heard erupting down on the streets as drive bys and shoots outs are occurring, fighting for territory. Little Ki Ki processing her thoughts on what King Black just said about the Mendez twins rating and still pushing product, even hitting him up on the phone pressed to move product they're getting stuck with since her arrival back on the scene.

"Say man, tell them rat ass niggas you ready for them". Little Ki Ki said.

"Then what? We can't do this shit here in the towers, that shit will blow back on me". King Black responded, thinking about how this shit is going down. It can't be done here because the cartel would come for him. He didn't want that type of blow back. Even with his gang being violent and ready to ride out, the cartel would come to massacre.

"We meet them outside of ya hood, me and my YG niggas will handle the rest". Little Ki Ki said with this vengeful look in her eyes, feeling the betrayal of the code of the streets as well as this next level lifestyle they're in.

"Aight, I got you". King Black responded making the call, setting the meeting place.

"Say man do they both show up or just one of them?" Little Ki Ki asked.

"They only trust each other, so they stick together". King Black responded thinking about how this shit is going down. "If you don't kill them, this shit ain't going to go right. They're going to want blood in return, especially with me putting this shit in play". He added.

"Don't worry my nigga, this ain't about no talking to see why they ratted. I'm a rock them bitch ass niggas to sleep with bullets ". Little Ki Ki stated angered and hyped to take care of this. The more she thought about how them snitching, creating a domino effect, taking out her, TK, Suga Baby and Red Rain, even La Vieja, who would have had them murdered cartel style, had she not got hit by M-13. For Ki Ki she just want to set eyes on them, so they can see her murderous rage, as she pulls the trigger over and over into their faces.

Within forty five minutes, they were at Crown Fried Chicken on the corner, a few blocks away from the towers. Carlos and Christian Mendez pulled up in a brand-new cranberry red bullet proof G55 AMG Mercedes Benz truck parking directly in front of the Crown Fried Chicken. Carlos calling up King Black, seeing if he's inside. "What up Los?"

"Amigo, we're are you?"

"I'm sitting in here with my niggas fucking this fried chicken up".

"We out front".

"Come on inside, treat yourself to some of the best fried chicken in the city. I'll buy you some of them spicy wings. After we're done we talk business". King Black said coming to the door way with a fried drum stick in his hand, taking a bite of it, before gesturing for them to come in. King Black never seen this truck they're driving, however he knew it was them, being the bosses they are. The passenger side tinted window came down revealing Christian's face. Both twins having a bald fade cut close on top, full beards shaped with razor perfection, just as their eyebrows, allowing their grey eyes to stand out luring women in.

"We don't have time to be eating chicken!" Christian stated firmly looking on at King Black. King Black still eating the remaining drum stick as he walk over to the truck, coming up to the door looking inside of the truck seeing two exotic females looking like social media influencers all dolled up, ready to ball out with these two king pins.

"You two pretty mutha fuckas is distracted with these exotic bitches, when you should be focusing on getting this paper". King Black said trying to change their minds to come inside. Christian brought into view a Mac-11 fully automatic with a fifty round clip one in the chamber, ready to roll.

"We're always about business. Like these bitches in the back seat, that fried chicken shit can wait". Christian said, before lowering the gun, at the same time King Black tossed the chicken to the curb.

"Let me get my shit inside". King Black said, going back inside of the chicken spot, over to the table with the bag of money. Little Ki Ki along with six YG young bucks was inside, strapped and ready to rock out.

"Them pretty niggas don't want to get out of the truck. They got these bitches in the back they showing off for. So I'm a go out with the bag, make the switch then you get at them rat ass niggas". King Black said before heading back outside totting the duffle bag. Christian rolled the window back up before exiting with the Mac-11 in hand safety off, one in the chamber. He walk to the back side of the truck, opening it up, revealing two bags of kilos.

"Next time we do business, be ready, time is money". Christian said.

"It looks more like I'm cutting into you and your twin brothers freak show with them exotic bitches".

"Oye hermano heads up policia". Carlos yelled out telling his brother to be cautious, seeing a cop car coming down the street.

Each of them now locked on the approaching cop car. At the same time Christian is closing the back of the truck, securing the money. King Black turned walking away seeing the YG niggas and Little Ki Ki exiting fast out of the chicken spot, guns at the ready. Their fast movement caught Christian's eye, he turned towards them raising the Mac-11 simultaneously to them taking aim, with no regard or awareness of the approaching cop car. Gunfire erupted from the Mac-11 spraying, gunning down two of the YG young bucks. At the same time, the others returned fire, including Little Ki Ki running towards Christian, pulling the trigger on Christian's falling body, filling him up with slugs from her new 10mm all black Colt. Each slug sucking the life from his flesh. The cop's siren and lights flipped on as he radioed in for back up, notifying dispatch of this shoot out. Carlos, not caring hit the switch on the passenger window, spraying bullets at the YGs seeing they gunned his brother down. The girls in the back seat are screaming, in fear for their lives, not realizing they're inside of a bullet proof truck. Carlos rolled the window back up when he seen Little Ki Ki running towards him, taking aim to unload the entire clip into the window. All to no avail, each slug being stopped by the layered bullet proof glass. She figured this out quick. Wishing she could have got his bitch ass outside of the truck like his twin. Now she has to figure out how she's going to get at him after tonight, because he's definitely going to be on high alert, may be even moving with a team of goons after this.

"Yo lets get the fucka out of here!" Little Ki Ki yelled out to the YG niggas that's still standing. The downed YGs that loss their lives, their families will be looked out for. She'll give Bundles money for their funerals and families. Little Ki Ki and the other YGs all took off running making their escape. Carlos not giving a fuck about the cop, mashed the gas taking off daring the cop to chase behind him. At this point he would bang it out with them, until his last breath or bullet to the face. Losing his twin brother is burning him deep, making him want revenge on Little Ki Ki, especially seeing her face charging towards him. He'll never forget her face, or give up tracking her down to avenge his twin brother, by any means necessary, it's murder season, cartel style.

Chapter 7

A few days later in Illinois over at the federal correctional facility. The federal government is preparing to transfer Red Rain and Suga Baby over to Pennsylvania. The Dauphin County Sheriff's Department is coming to get both of them, having made an agreement with the Atlanta Police Department to pick Red Rain up before passing her onto them for attempted homicide on a officer from Dauphin County. So for the sheriffs department it was a pleasure for them to pick these two female gangsters up, so they both can be officially arraigned and charged for homicide and attempted homicide.

"We're here to pick up two for transport for Dauphin County. Shandrea Richards and Keisha Jackson". Sheriff Rolstien said into the intercom awaiting to be buzzed into the secured sally port. The buzzard sounded off as the spike tracks lowered into the ground to prevent puncture of the tires. The door raised up, allowing the sheriffs to enter. The car drove in, stopping where the federal guard halted them. Then another armed guard came over to the car as the window came down, as instructed by the sign in front of them.

"Let me see your paperwork ". The federal guard said, while the other guards stood at the ready, having high level criminals and masterminds attempt pay officers to break them out before. Especially high ranking cartel members. So now they remain on high alert never trusting anyone, coming in or out of the prison. The paper work is good he took the paper to the control booth placing it in the bubble so the higher ranking guard can pass the info on to the guards inside the prison, to pack these women up. The guard came back to the sheriffs.

"They'll be out in a little. You men brought your own shackles and cuffs?"

"Yes we have everything we need". The sheriff responded.

"All right, step out of the car, check your weapons over at the control. Then take your shackles and cuffs inside the reception where you'll secure them and receive your paperwork".

They did as instructed, seeing how meticulously secured this facility is. When Suga Baby and Red Rain came down to the reception area seeing the sheriffs, all hopes of being set free went out of the door. Each of them was told they're leaving, not that the sheriffs is waiting on them.

"This is some bull shit. They could let us stay here and do our time, instead of moving us around again". Red Rain said, not liking that they're being uprooted again.

"Turn around and raise your feet up". The sheriff said securing the shackles. He did the same for both women, before taking them out to the car, securing them in the back seat. Then they grabbed their weapons before exiting heading back to Pennsylvania. "I hope you ladies used

56

the bathroom, because it won't be any stops, other than for food". The fat sheriff in the passenger seat said, then added. "I don't want any shit out of you two either. I heard you pretty bitches are deadly".

"Fuck you, fat bastard!" Suga Baby fired back.

"You better be glad it wasn't you chasing behind us, or we would have popped your fat ass". Red Rain added. The sheriff driving smirked at how feisty these two are.

"All right ladies, bring it down a notch, listen to some music, it's going to be a long drive". He said turning the XM radio up playing Liquid Octane. Both ladies looking at each other, before shaking their heads, thinking this is going to be torture, especially not being fans of heavy metal.

A few hours into the drive, they pulled into a rest stop. One by one the sheriffs went to use the bathroom. Along with grabbing food for themselves and the ladies. Once they were done, they started back towards Harrisburg, Pennsylvania, the capitol of PA.

"Hey". Red Rain said in a low tone, having this look on his face that Suga Baby picked up on.

"What?" Suga Baby asked. Red Rain looked behind them, seeing this black Chevy Tahoe that has been following them for close to two hours. They got off at the exit at the rest stop when they did, they never exited the truck at the rest stop, only waited for them to get mobile again. Soon as Suga Baby looked back, the Tahoe sped up going around the sheriff's car.

"You trippen babe". Suga Baby said down playing Red Rain's paranoia.

Suddenly, shifting their attention, the sheriff blurted out.

"What the hell is this!?" Both Red Rain and Suga Baby turned forward, seeing a mask man out the back of the Tahoe tossing a spike strip in front of the sheriff's car, going under puncturing the tires, running them flat. At the same time the Tahoe is slowing down, forcing the sheriff's car to come to a slow halt.

"Call it in! We're being attacked!" Sheriff Rolstein yelled out, trying to control the car with the flattened tires. The car stopping no longer able to move. Each sheriff shocked, by what's taking place, never having gained for this. Each of them fumbling for their side arms, as three men exited in all black fatigues from the Tahoe, clearly with trained precision weapons aimed as they moved in with M4 assault rifles, with suppressors and red laser beams on them. The sheriffs still trying to raise their weapons, until gunfire erupted slamming into their vest.

"Don't be a hero, the next rounds will be in your faces, so let this just happen, so you make it home to your loved ones". The lead trained ex-Navy Seal said, as the sheriffs struggled to breathe from the slugs crashing into their vest. The point was made, they wouldn't make any more attempts to stop what's taking place, especially overwhelmed by fear and the skills before them. These men were contract by TK thanks to Salvator's deep rooted connections. Sal also informed TK to pay and only use them once, because they've been known to cancel the contractor, to prevent any trace of who they are. The trained men closed in shattering the windows, extracting both of the ladies, who didn't hesitate to go with them fearing they too would be shot. What they didn't know is who is behind this, or if they would be killed once they reached their destination with these mask men. The sheriffs looked on helpless as the mask men removed the women from their custody with ease. Each of the women looking on at how precise and trained these men are moving, taking them to the truck, before tossing a few smoke canisters on the road creating thick clouds of smoke, preventing any movement distorting and or blinding oncoming traffic, the sheriff's car, even the Tahoe. By the time the cans of smoke stop spraying allowing the smoke to dissipate, the Tahoe was long gone, to their secondary vehicle, then to the airport where they gave both women a secured package with things they need during and after their flight to Florida, where TK is expecting them in his new mansion. Neither of the women questioned these trained men about their destination or who these men work for. For them they are now free and soon to be far away from a jail cell and a life bid.

Chapter 8

When they finally landed in Miami, Florida with the sun shining, warm weather, they're feeling good, having a car awaiting them taking them to TK's ten thousand square foot mansion, secured by Fortress Elite Personal Security. A company recommended to him through Salvator. These men and women working for this company are all ex-military, trained around the world in all terrains. Now this next level of service protecting this home, property, its owner and occupants.

TK was inspired by the level of security and protection Hector has, so he wanted to achieve this same level of comfort his new fortune has afforded him, keeping in mind his position is what many strive and will kill for. Last he's checked, he's not moving over or out of the way for no one. The Maseratti truck pulled up to the large home on a few acres visibly secured. Both Red Rain and Suga Baby are unaware, who is responsible for getting them out. The masked men dropped them off, giving them plane tickets, instructions, before vanishing as fast as they came.

They exited the truck, walking up the steps leading to the double stained glass doors. Two Fortress security allowing them in, having already received info that TK would be expecting them. They can hear music playing as they entered, coming from the living room array. They followed the sounds of music. Soon as they entered the living room, they can see TK playing with junior, that's in his walker.

"Oh my God baby!" Suga Baby said breaking down crying running over to her son, she's missed and dreamed of for what seems like forever to a mother. She started hugging and kissing junior on his chubby cheeks. Red Rain came over embracing TK with love and appreciation.

"Thank you for not forgetting us". Red Rain said, becoming emotional, tears of love and happiness coming down her face. Suga Baby picking her son up giving him hugs, love and kisses.

"You going to make me wait for my hug, kisses and thank you?" TK said being funny.

"I'm sorry babe, I love you so much for this. Me and Rain will thank you later, because we miss your wood and the excitement you bring into our lives and bodies". Suga Baby said giving TK a kiss and hug as they all came together for one loving embrace.

"I had a stylist go shopping for y'all, so after you shower, you'll have the finest and sexiest shit to wear, then at the end of the night, I'll do the honors in taking it all off". TK said making them smile wanting him sexually even more.

"We love and appreciate you more than anything, but you know the feds and cops is going to be looking for us heavy". Red Rain said thinking back to how these trained men broke them out of police custody.

"I have something in play as we speak. Shit is different for us now, in case you haven't noticed. I met the direct

62

connect, Hector Sanchez. That mutha fucka got a different type of power. He got people that got people for any and everything. We have access to it all as long as that paper flows with no excuses". TK said before going into detail about how La Vieja set in place insurance that made it all possible for him to be out, so he put insurance on them to get them out. "Now until I get things situated for you and Rain, y'all have to stay in the house or on the property. You two will figure out how to have fun, plus junior will keep you busy. Right now go get showered and dressed, I have the chef making us a good dinner". TK said taking his son, giving each of them a kiss before watching them head up the steps in the grey sweat suits the mask men gave them. They took the jail uniforms they had, placing them on the dead bodies of two females close to their ages, weight and race. Then they staged a car crash that ended in a engulfing flame, that only leaves traces of their inmate IDs, clothing, handcuffs and shackles. The news outlets covered the story, painting the picture of a prisoner breakout that turned deadly for the prisoners, that tried to get away, only to Suga Baby said with a salacious smile and eyes, biting her lip seductively.

"If I didn't have patience, I would oblige, but right now I'm focused". He responded. The staff came with drinks, already knowing what each lady prefers thanks to TK filling them in.

"I do have some more good news for y'all two sexy beast. While y'all was in the shower, News Nation reported Shandrea Richards and Keisha Jackson who broke out of police custody, died in a violent car crash, in what looks to be a stolen getaway car". TK said, taking his cell phone out, pulling up the news site showing it to them. Even social media is blasting it all over.

"This is some crazy shit bitch, they think we dead". Suga Baby said excited, feeling the weight lift from her body, of not having to look over her shoulders as before when she was running. Red Rain seemed to be speechless, knowing TK made this all possible with his new connection to the cartel. A true sacrifice for love. "We thank you for this babe". Suga Baby said seeing the emotions in Rain's eyes.

"I know you appreciate this. Nothing will come between family and I mean this". TK said removing two velvet red jewelry boxes with Provident Jeweler imprinted on them. "What we have is real, it's different and unconventional, just like this proposal of me asking you two ride or die bitches, to love each other and me until our last breath. This bond right here is bigger than marriage. These five carat solitary diamonds set in platinum is how I want to express my commitment in return for your sacrifice, love and loyalty". TK said standing to put the rings on each of their fingers, followed by passionate kisses from each of them. Both of them in joyful tears, staring at the flawless diamonds.

"We fucking your face and body all night babe, to show you are appreciation". Suga Baby said. They all erupted with laughter, at the same time looking toward to how this night is going to end. Sweet sweat, heated passionate, I love you forever sex.

"One more thing. I can't forget the little hommie". TK said hitting up Little Ki Ki on the face time. She picked up quick seeing who it is.

"What it do folk?"

64

"I just put the family back together. Keep that on the low with all the chatter going around". TK said handing the phone to Suga Baby. She took the phone showing off her ring, then Red Rain's ring.

"Two rings for two bad bitches". Suga Baby said, turning the phone camera on herself. Shocking little Ki Ki.

"Yo this shit is crazy. They saying you and shawty burnt up, dead and gone ya hear me?"

"That's how we going to leave it too. Only you and us know the truth. I am glad to see you bitch, when you coming this way? Oh how's sexy ass Karin doing?"

"I'll be that way after I secure shit up here. You know with this team expansion, we have to keep it tight ya feel me? As for Karin, I'll have to put you up on how that situation went face to face, not over the line like that".

"Ki Ki we love you bitch for holding us down and riding with us in the joint". Red Rain said from the side as Suga Baby held the phone so they both can be in view.

"We family, it's what we do out here. We all we got in this game". Ki Ki said meaning it. TK and the ladies are all Ki Ki have. No real family, having been raised in foster care, which made her as hard as she is.

"We can't wait for you to come down here, so we can be a family. Plus junior has gotten big, missing his aunty sis". Red Rain said.

"Yeah you already. I'm a have to get little man something from up this way so he can stunt on all the little babies down there".

"Aight, baby girl talk to you later". Suga Baby said ending the call. The food came, they enjoyed fresh lobster, steak, prongs with garnish and sides. Red wine, followed by shots of Hennessey, enjoying the evening, each others time, laughter and conversation, while appreciating the true love and romance between them. Each of them feeling on top of the world in this relationship, the game and love.

"Raise your glasses, this is a toast to our family, this love, new start, and staying in power". TK said. " Don't forget, to a night of unforgettable love making ". Red Rain added, looking intimately into his eyes. They toast their glasses, embracing this moment of power and love. TK placed a passionate kiss on Red Rain's lips, warming her heart and body, igniting all she's yearned for since the day of her arrest. Their hands roaming over each other's bodies, undressing one another, leading up the stairs, even Suga Baby in the intimate mix, finding their way to the bedroom, where the power of erotic passion, erupted, stimulating their bodies, hearts and minds in every way. Taking this love and relationship to the next level, the more their sweet sweating flesh intertwined with one another. Each touch seeming to melt away as orgasmic sensations stirred, racing through their bodies and hearts, with each stroke and switching of positions. The intense intimate, erotic session lasted into the late hours of the night as if they were all making love for the last time, or for the first time, chasing that good, good feeling of powerful orgasms erupting over and over, until they fell asleep in each others comfort, feeling on top of the world.

The Crown Is Mine

Chapter 9

A few weeks after being technically dead to the world, due to a violent car crash. Suga Baby and Red Rain received their new identifications, driver's license and passports. All thanks to TK's new position with access to unlimited resources.

Suga Baby's fake name is Patricia Davis, age twenty nine from Louisiana. She thought it was a crazy name, even Red Rain kept calling her Patty, knowing she didn't care for it. Red Rain's new name is Nikki Lambert from Tennessee, age twenty eight. Each of them was given a background story, to further back the new credentials. With this new lease on life and freedom. The ladies also changed their hair colors to look the part of the persons they're suppose to be. Suga Baby dyed her hair jet black, allowing her smooth skin and facial features to stand out. She even got grey eye contacts, adding to the look. Red Rain dyed her hair white blond, making her look more white, allowing her biracial features come out, both of them dyed their eyebrows the color of their new hair.

Now with their new look, they wanted new clothes, so they went out shopping for the finest fashions, accompanied by four of the Fortress security guards, following behind them in a white Yukon Denalis. Red Rain drove the white pearl Rolls Royce Wraith, with charcoal a grey strip on the hood, adding to the prestigious look to this up scale luxury coupe. They pulled up to the block of designer stores and celebrity owned fashion boutiques. TK made sure they had enough cash money to spoil themselves with. Each of them now exiting the Wraith, already looking like stars, with their five carat flawless solitary engagement rings, sparkling as much as their glow of being free, backed by the memorable night of erotic love and passion, that's permeating through their smiles and glow. They entered the store displaying beauty, power and presence. All things that got them immediate assistance from the store's stylist, when they entered the store.

"Ladies, welcome to Global Designs, if you don't see what you're looking for we can place a order direct from the runways in Milan, Asia, Dubai or wherever the designer is you're looking for". The female stylist said, runway ready herself with the latest Dolce & Gabanna.

"We're just trying to make our man happy, keeping it sexy and fashionable at all times". Suga Baby said. The stylist noticing the matching solitary diamond engagement rings, along with their security, so she knew they came to spend big.

"Everything you see here is fresh off of the runway, you'll be the first and may be the only to have it".

"We got it from here". Red Rain said, not needing a stylist, plus she could see it in her eyes that she's chasing the commission of sale, knowing they're big spenders. They ladies continued on for close to a hour, shopping getting all they liked, and felt they would look sexy and cute in. Spending close to sixty thousand in high end designers, mainly one of a kind looks, so they don't see another bitch copying their style. They brought all of their things to the counter, to ring it up, excited about how their shopping day has went us far, until they heard two females behind them smacking their teeth. Suga Baby glanced over her shoulder at the Italian females staring back at them. The one having dark hair, blonde highlights, heavy makeup, covering their Miami tanned skin. Each of the females looking to be in their twenties, or younger. In here spending their daddies money. "Don't be hating, our money spends just like your daddies money". Suga Baby said as she placed ten grand stacks all hundred dollar bills, to pay for their clothing.

"I seen your kind before, that money don't last. But daddy's money do". The Italian female said flipping out her dad's American Express Black Card. " No limit, I can buy the store if I like". She added.

"Say shawty, what you mean your kind? Bitch I will slap you and that black card around!" Red Rain snapped, angered by these two snobby bitches. The other female removing her cell phone, starting to record now sensing hostility that they created. At the same time she started commentating as she recorded.

"This is what happens when these people get money. They want to buy up everything being in our way, like we don't have places to go and money to spend elsewhere". Red Rain snapped, taking the Gucci handbag smacking the girl holding the phone with the handbag, jolting her. She still gripped the phone really in fear.

"Oh my God! This frign muli just hit me with that expensive hand bag. See America, what a waste". Suga

Baby showing the other female the handle of her gun she pulled from her Prada clutch.

"You should know better to talk to strangers, with this level of disrespect. You think your money and white privilege makes you safe out here? There's not enough makeup to fix the bullet holes I'll put in your face". Suga Baby said giving the other girl this dark murderous stare, shaking her to the core.

"I'm sorry. I didn't mean anything by it. Can you please tell your friend to stop, she's hurting her". The female said, seeing Red Rain stomping the Italian girl with the arrogant mouth. The heel of her Vera Wang shoes piercing the flesh.

"That bitch had enough". Suga baby said to Red Rain, at the same time tossing an additional ten grand on the counter top, before grabbing their things. The security following out, making sure neither girl retaliated. While they prepared to jump in their car, the female shouted out, snapping on the store employees.

"I'm going to sue this fucking place! You have wild people like that attacking people of class like animals! It's all on video too! Do you know who my father is!?" The shaken girl shouted, helping the other girl up, seeing the blood on her face from the puncture in her cheek from the heel.

"Ma'am we called the police if you want to file a report". The manager said, wanting to appease the customer.

Back outside of the store, Red Rain took her bloody heels off, before getting into the Rolls Royce Wraith, then she tossed the shoes into one of the shopping bags after she dumped the clothes in the back seat.

"Them bitches got what they deserve acting all snobby and shit". Red Rain said still feeling her anger and adrenaline flowing.

"They think they better than us because we look different. I wasn't feeling that type of disrespect shawty".

"I was about to pistol whip that other bitch, since she's the one that set it off talking shit, plus she was looking like she was about to jump in, until I flash that heat". Suga Baby said, as they drove back to the mansion. The two girls at the store, filed a report to the cops when they showed up, accompanied by the store footage and the other girl's cell phone footage. Each of them playing the victim as if this was a spontaneous act, and they didn't know why it took place. The police didn't buy that part, however they have to proceed with what they have, tracking these two suspects down to get their side and make a arrest. The store staff also backing these two young white girls, fearing a law suit as she threatened, along with repercussions from the Italian Mafia. Victoria and Priscilla Coviello are the daughters and Frank Coviello, and the grand daughters of New York Crime Boss Don Carmine Coviello. Made men or not, the mafia crime family would not tolerate or allow this level of disrespect towards any of its family members or associates.

Chapter 10

Within a few hours, the incident at Global Designs, has spread fast through the local Miami news, social media, with everyone having their own opinions, hash tags, good and bad. This incident as told to TK by Red Rain and Suga Baby, isn't as the video and social media has it playing out. Especially with the media making references to the Coviello Crime Family. TK didn't go through all of this to break them free, getting new fake identities, faking their deaths, all for them to fuck this shit up. TK being focused on business, keeping Hector in mind. Knowing he doesn't accept any excuses when it comes to getting his money or moving his product.

"I can't believe this shit! Y'all done fucked up, having your faces on blast, acting stupid and shit!" TK vented, pacing back and forth in the living room, looking up at the 60 inch float screen looping the feed of what took place at the store.

"She was trippen babe, like we wasn't suppose to be there". Suga Baby said.

"Fuck what they think! We out here getting this next level money. Nothing or no one stands in the way of that!" He expressed firmly, love aside in this level of business, because that is one excuse that will get you killed.

He cares for them deeply, they have a unbreakable bond, but when it comes to fucking this money up, he can't have that. Nothing can fuck with Hector's money or shipments.

For TK, he loves his money and new position of power more than he loves these women. TK knows it won't be long before the cops come seeking to arrest them, ruining all he sacrificed using his assets given to him from Salvator. As these thoughts are entering his mind, his cell phone sounded off, followed by a member of the Fortress Security coming in.

"Sir we have officers at the front gate coming to the house". The security said, at the same time TK answered his secured phone.

"What's good?"

"I don't know, you tell me. I received a call from an associate that handled the paperwork and he tells me it's been ruined already. What is that all about?" Salvator asked, clearly upset that his resources has been misused and abused. Salvator is more than a lawyer TK has long figured that out. He's well connected globally and not to be fucked with, no matter how calm and professional he remains at all times. Sal is the guy that can get you anything from a Picasso to drones armed with whatever you want. You need to vanish, he'll ask how and when, because he is always a phone call away from a guy that could take care of any and all he request. He's well traveled, globally known and respected in the underground world.

The Crown Is Mine

"I understand that's not a good look for any of us. I'll handle it. I'm checking the details now". TK responded feeling the let down, with using Salvator's resources.

"Aye all emotions aside, I do have a guy that can clean that up for you, so it doesn't effect this business of ours, forcing you to run into excuses that aren't accepted. You know what I mean?" Sal said referring to having someone take the women out. As mad as TK is with them right now, he couldn't authorize that. Even if Sal views them as a liability. For Sal he didn't want to expose his resources that broke them out of prison, or got TK off, even faking their deaths. If exposed a lot of fingers can be pointed in directions that can destroy and empire. Mainly with the federal government who will not sleep, trying to figure out who is powerful enough to pull this off, and why? TK didn't want to respond aggressive or emotional, as he's thinking and feeling, allowing his emotions to get in the way, to protect his women.

"Any decision I make in this business is never emotional. I'll take care of my end, assuring there will be no excuses or obstacles in my way".

"Don't be frign stubborn, if you know what's good for you. I'll be keeping a close eye on this thing. If it's not to our liking, I won't be as courteous, giving you this option ". Salvator said before ending the call.

TK is feeling disrespected, along with pressure of handling this since it was caught on camera and phone video, being streamed over and over on-line.

"Go upstairs, while I deal with these cops". TK directed Suga Baby and Red Rain, staring at them, visibly pissed, having so many thoughts of his world as he envisioned it all falling apart.

Suga Baby haven't seen this look in his eyes in almost two years when he kicked in Big Butch's front door gunning everyone down in the house, except for her and Tati. This look scared her then, even more now, sending confusion in her heart and mind, especially with them having a child together. TK came to the front porch of the mansion, seeing two squad cars pulling into his driveway. He also noticed a unmarked car that pulled up on the outside the driveway. Not good. He's thinking, knowing the likelihood of them being feds or detectives. Either one, is not good for him, his new home or business. The officers exited their vehicles seeing the Fortress Security around the home, along with two of them at TK's side.

"Gentlemen, how can I help you this evening?" TK said, switching the tone of his voice to a more professional upscale tone.

"Mr. King, do you own a Rolls Royce Wraith sir?" The officer asked having retrieved the video footage from Global Design's outside cameras, which lead them to trace to gave and registration to his home. He figured this out, since the fake names the ladies have wouldn't have lead the police here.

"Yes I do, would you like to purchase it?" He said being funny, knowing the officer couldn't afford it if they all chipped in.

"These two females drove away in your car after a crime was committed". The officer said.

"What? A crime? No wonder they dropped the car off without saying anything before they left". TK said playing along as if he was the victim, being used by these women.

"So you know these women?"

"Only their stripper names. I was drinking last night at King of Diamonds, having fun, the one girl's name is Gia, she was all over me. When I woke up they were gone. My security guy told me they had another girl come pick them up". TK said lying, but sounding truthful.

"King of Diamonds huh?" The officer responded. "I guess that's our only lead now guys. Thank you for your time Mr. King".

"You're welcome, anything I can do to keep us protected out here". TK responded as they walked away getting into their cars driving off. Now that's out of the way, he has to figure out exactly who is in that unmarked car, outside of his driveway. He turned to his security guy on his right. "I want you to find out who is in that car, why they're sitting outside of my driveway and why the front gate let them in?"

"Yes sir I'm on it". The security said radioing in to his team over the earpiece. They closed in quick on the car, only to discover it's two FBI agents, from the Miami office, that was called on behalf of the FBI office in Georgia, who originally took TK, Suga Baby, Red Rain, and Little Ki Ki down. Agent Pedro Morales, like the rest of the social media onlookers, seen the store brawl. Agent Morales didn't buy into the deaths of Keisha Jackson or Shandrea Richards. In fact he made a call to Pennsylvania's FBI to have the bodies checked for dental records, and compare them to what they have on file. Agent Morales sent these agents out to physically set eyes on the women he believes are Shandrea Richards and Keisha Jackson.

"Sir the men are federal agents. We noticed their credentials along with running the tag". The security said to TK adding to his anger and pressure of this situation that is getting out of control fast. This situation will also put the spot light on him now with the feds being curious of this staged death. His movements will be monitored. TK headed up to the second floor where the ladies are.

"I spent the cops, but we have a new problem. The feds was also out there sitting on the edge of my driveway.

I want both of y'all to leave the city and east coast for awhile. You can take junior with you. Go to a small town, no big cities, no being flash, loud or arrogant. Don't draw any attention to yourselves. Tone everything about you down, if you want to be free and be a family". TK said.

"You want us to be some regular bitches huh?" Red Rain asked, then added "That hoe shouldn't have been popping off at the mouth".

"Babe, please let us stay here, we won't leave the house. I just want to be a family with all of us". Suga Baby pleaded, feeling her heart being tugged by this decision of being apart from all she loves all over again.

"This isn't just about you being regular bitches or breaking our family up. This is me, protecting all I love. I told y'all before, we on some next level business, where there is no excuses, no liabilities. A lot went into getting y'all right here, and you fucked it up. That shit looks bad on me, at the same time, I'm responsible to make sure this situation is resolved". TK stated trying to clue them in on how real this shit is. If it was up to Salvator, they would be dead by the morning, or gone without a trace.

"No matter what, we love you TK". Suga Baby said, reminding him of their love and loyalty.

"I don't doubt that at all, but I have to protect this love and family we have. When it's clear out there my security will take y'all to where you need to go. Once shit gets quiet again, I'll reach out to y'all". He said bringing them close, for an embrace that is feeling like their last. The women without saying it, can feel it in their hearts and body.

Chapter 11

9:07 AM Suga Baby, TK and Red Rain finished up what breakfast they could eat, knowing they would have to part for a little while, until things died down. They all stood from the dining table, coming together for a emotional embrace.

"We love you so much babe. I'll send you pictures of junior every day, so you won't miss him or us". Suga Baby said.

"I love you and Rain, but don't go to South Dakota acting like fools. Pierre being the capitol, it's a good low key spot for y'all to be for six months, then move to Odgen, Utah another lay low area, before sliding back this way". He said before kissing each of them with love and passion. Then he gave his son, a big hug and kiss. "I'm a miss you little big man. Keep mom and Aunt Shandrea in line out there". TK said, handing junior to Suga Baby as he walk them out to the truck with his security awaiting them. They would escort them to the airport, then return back to the mansion.

What the ladies didn't know or notice, two plain clothed FBI agents also boarded the flight with them, wanting to see where they're going. Also to see if they're moving large sums of money or drugs in the half dozen

LV designer suitecases. The FBI agents were also awaiting official confirmation that these two females are definitely their escaped fugitives, and not the women they're losing as on their new identifications. Close to four hours passed by before they landed in Pierre, South Dakota. As they were exiting the plane, going through the airport, a voice called out to them.

"Excuse me ma'am, is this your son's diaper bag?" Suga Baby hearing this stopped, looking back, seeing this man approaching with her Gucci diaper bag. She smiled, glad he was nice enough to bring it to her, especially with the cash money under the diapers and baby wipes.

"Thank you so much, that was nice of you". Suga Baby said.

"No problem. I know how it is being in a hurry, running wild". He said giving a brief smile before adding, " Are you two like famous singers or reality TV stars?"

"No, we're regular people". Red Rain responded looking on at him with his creepy stare.

"You sure? I feel like I've seen you before". He insisted, looking over at his partner on the phone.

Red flags and fear shot spiked, placing Red Rain on high alert. Suga Baby also followed his eyes to see who he is looking at. At the same time fear shooting through her, feeling helpless not having weapons or their security with them, to stand their ground.

"Nikki let's go". Suga Baby called out to Red Rain, in a tone that raised her sense even more. She hurried to her side walking away in between looking back at the man they were talking to. He's now talking to someone.

"I hope this creepy mutha fucka wasn't trying to snatch us". Red Rain said, thinking the two men are predators. "They cops bitch, probably feds. They've been following us". Suga Baby stated, walking fast holding onto junior with a motherly embrace, wanting to protect him by never being apart from him ever again. Red Rain looking back noticing they not following them.

"They're not following us anymore. You probably overreacted bitch". Red Rain said. Suga Baby stopped, turning to look at Rain.

"I'm not trippen bitch. It's called instinct, and that shit didn't feel right back there. I'm not going to jail or being apart from my baby again. We're on the next flight out of this city and state. We stand out here to LA, in the hood where we belong and wont stand out". Suga Baby said heading to baggage claims to get their things before looking for a new flight.

"The next flight out is in fifteen minutes. I'll process your luggage. Your terminal is 17E". The lady at the counter said to them handing over the new tickets. Outside of the airport the two federal agents, now having confirmation that Patricia Davis is Keisha Jackson. Nikki Lambert is Shandrea Richards. This info was sent to Agent Morales in Georgia, from the Pennsylvania office, then he relayed it to Agents Smalls and Douglas. Now they're outside of the airport, awaiting the two females to exit. They even called for local and federal law enforcement for assistance, so they can be housed over night at one of their facilities, once apprehended. Agent Smalls a white male with a close marine style hair cut, clan shaven in shape, standing six foot even. Driven and focused on being the best agent he can be at all times, doing everything by the book. His partner is the nerdy Agent Douglas, having buck teeth, glasses, precise with all he does by the numbers and statistics. Standing five foot seven, short hair buzzed close on the sides. He's also the one that made first contact with Suga Baby and Red Rain, which they viewed him as creepy. Agent Douglas is looking on at his watch in between adjusting his glasses with his index finger. Then he's looking up at the dual sliding doors at the front entrance, parting each time thinking these pretty female goons are coming through. His partner also looking at how he's anticipating these women coming out.

"Agent Smalls by the numbers give or take with the bathroom break, they should have been out here a minute and thirty seconds ago".

"She has a baby too. She could be changing the child's shitty diaper. Good thing for you didn't leave the bag on the plane". Agent Smalls responded.

"Okay, okay, adding baby into the equation. We should wait another two minutes, three tops for diaper change". Agent Douglas stated, keeping a eye on his watch and the sliding doors. "Time!" Agent Douglas yelled out exactly three minutes later. Agent Smalls laughed at his partner keeping time like it's a boxing match, yelling out time. "Something isn't right, they should be out here by now. All of the exits are secured, covered by agents and local law enforcement". Agent Douglas stated before walking back inside of the airport, looking around, then rushing over to baggage claim No LV designed luggage or the women in sight. He rushed to

The Crown Is Mine

the bathrooms, checking them, not even caring if females blurted obscenities at him. His focus is catching wanted women, who escaped custody to evade federal and state charges. Agent Douglas' fast thinking, went to the ticket counter, showing his federal credentials to expedite the process. He also presented pictures of both women. "Did you see these two women come through here with a baby boy?" The lady behind the counter zoomed in on the photos.

"What's their names?" She asked.

"The names they booked a flight from Miami to Pierre is, Nikki Lambert and Patricia Davis". Agent Douglas responded, sounding anxious, displaying urgency in his tone. The clerk raced her fingers fast tapping in the info given.

"These ladies booked a flight to LA. The plane is on the runway preparing for takeoff".The clerk said.

"We need that plane grounded now!" Agent Douglas stated firmly.

"I'll get the other agents and officers to assist". Agent Smalls said.

The clerk radioed in to her superiors connecting the federal agent to the plane on the runway, to halt it temporarily, so they get secure the two wanted women. Close to two dozen squad cars, agents and airport security, raced out to the now stationary 737 jumbo passenger jet, that's lined up for takeoff. The pilot now can see the fast approaching vehicles and flashing lights. The airport staff brought steps to the plane allowing the federal agents access inside of the plane, looking for their wanted suspects. They swept through the plane, going to the seats

85

assigned to them. Not them, only a elder couple looking up at the agents in confusion of why they're standing over them looking so serious. In this very moment, they're all feeling duped, the women never got on the plane, thanks to Red Rain's fast thinking, knowing if they made it to LAX, the feds would be there when they landed. They got a rental car, heading to their new destination, a city they can hide. They also have to let TK know what went down, so he won't mad at them.

Chapter 12

Within a few hours after being duped by Suga Baby and Red Rain, Agents Smalls and Douglas called the media, so they can put both females on blast, making them feel the pressure, exposing them faking their deaths, while still being wanted.

"I'm Federal Agent Smalls, this is my partner Agent Douglas. On behalf of the Georgia and Pennsylvania federal offices, we were able to discover Keisha 'Suga Baby' Jackson, along with Shandrea 'Red Rain' Richards are both alive and well. Having broke out of police custody with the help of trained men as reported by the Dauphin County Sheriff's Department. The fake crash was also staged to further the deception of the demise of these women. If it wasn't for the social media footage, this would have never been discovered. These women are traveling with a child using the alias names, Patricia Davis, and Nikki Lambert. Anyone who see these women, we ask that you call the FBI number at the bottom of your screen. There is a five hundred thousand dollar reward". Agent Smalls said, now feeling a sense of relief, having got this info out to the public, making America a small place for them to hide.

As he was speaking, the news outlets are showing multiple pictures of each woman, ranging from arrest photos to Red Rain's Instagram and Twitter accounts. This national news also reaching TK, angering him knowing he would here from his associates about how this is all gone way too far. Especially the mention of trained men getting them out, coupled with staging their deaths in the car crash. This level of expertise will without a doubt raise questions. Questions TK nor his associates will take a liking to.

"I can't believe this shit!" TK yelled out looking on at the large screen TV with Suga Baby and Red Rain's pictures. TK's cell phone sounded off shifting his attention to it. It's the little hommie Ki Ki. "Yo what's good with you?"

"Say man, what they done got themselves into?"

"Some shit that can't be fixed or undone".

He responded, crushed by it all knowing what he sacrificed to bring them together, has been tossed away, because of the store incident. Now they'll never be together as family with this amount of exposure they're getting. Even with Salvator's connections, he wouldn't be able to do it, because Sal being a man of business will view them as a liability. Right now they are.

"Say man, you need to get junior away from that chaos ya feel me? He don't need to be around that, in case shit don't go right ya hear me?" Little Ki Ki said.

TK feeling her words, knowing they wouldn't go down easy, it would be a gunfight his son doesn't need to be around.

"I'm already thinking about that. I'm a hit you back, I have to call them now".

"If you need me folk, say word and I'm there, ya feel me?" She said before hanging up. He hit up Suga Baby's phone. It rang a few times before she picked up.

"Please don't be mad babe. The feds was on the plane with us, we lost them switching flights, then getting a rental dodging them".

"Keisha, did you see the news, how they blasting y'all faces and real names? These mutha fuckas got a half a mil ticket on y'all head, to bring y'all in".

"We fucked up bad babe. You know I don't want to be apart from our son again, even if I have to run forever to keep him in my life. They won't find me or my son". Suga Baby said, not having any intentions of going to jail or separating from junior again.

"Keisha, when and wherever you find a place to hide, I'm coming for junior. If they bring harm to him, I'll never be able to forgive that". TK said firmly. She also knows he means every word of it.

"I'll call you when we get settled. We love you TK".

"I know, I just have to get control of this love, before it get us all killed or thrown in jail". He responded fully aware of the pros and cons of what they have between them, but at what cost is it worth holding onto. Red Rain took the phone from Suga Baby.

"TK I'll look after her and junior. I promise with my life on the line, because her love and your love is worth the sacrifice".

"Shandrea, like I told her, anything happens to my son, the earth is going to be scorched with a wrath of fire

89

I'm a set". His response didn't warrant a come back, so she hung up understanding every word. Suga Baby didn't have any intentions on parting from her son, even allowing TK to come get him. In doing so, she knows she would never physically see junior again, with her being on the run. Her position of fleeing would compromise all TK has with her coming around, so for her this is not an option, she'll never part from her son. Between her and Rain they have a million in cash, packed away in their LV designer luggage. Red Rain chose to head out to LA into the hood, where a lot of her IG and Twitter followers are. They would embrace her Lady boss gangsta, welcoming her into the hood. Before heading to the west coast, they switched cars, not wanting the rental to be linked to their path of travel.

Back on the east coast, TK is answering his phone with a call from Salvator.

"What's good with you?"

"Nothing is good my friend. Have you been watching the news?"

"Yeah, I addressed that issue already".

"Talking about is one thing, doing something about is another. That thing that was done, has been exposed. That's not good for the parties involved. They don't like when things fall apart, because their clients are careless. You know what I mean?"

"Sal, I got this under control over this way. Nothing, I mean nothing is going to fuck up what we have going. I don't care who it is, this money will be made". TK stated firmly, wanting to get his point across to be trusted, and nothing will come between them or their business.

90

"I hear your words my friend, just put that fire out before it spreads, all right?" Sal said meaning killing the women off.

"Say no more". TK would be faced with hard task, killing the two women he loves. Now he's rooting they never get caught, hiding even from him.

Chapter 13

Over a week passed by, TK loss contact with Suga Baby and Red Rain. This angered him since he was unable to at least speak with them. He also wanted to get his son away from them running. A part of him felt comfort knowing they went off the grid without a trace. Especially having found out mafia capo Frank Coviello and his mob goons were looking for Suga Baby and Red Rain to whack them. Frank wanted to set these mulis straight, with a bullet in both of their faces, for laying hands on his daughter.

"Mr. King, there's a Don Carmine Coviello at the gate wanting to speak with you". The lead security said. TK has heard about the mafia Don being the head of the five crime families in New York.

"Let him in, since he traveled all the way from New York, it must be important ". TK said still trippen how that incident has sparked this much problems, to bring a mafia Don to his home. TK's security searched the Don and the four mob goons he traveled with, removing all weapons before entering the mansion. The goons drove up in a black Lincoln Towne car, following behind the Don's rented Royal blue Bentley Flying Spur, with dark tinted windows. The Don along with his mafia goons are impressed with the level of security TK has, moving like Secret Service, taking their weapons before entering home.

"Don Coviello welcome to my home. Can my staff get you and your men anything?" TK asked, seeing how they I looking on at him like he's a street thing that doesn't deserve to live like this. TK didn't give a fuck what they thought of him, he was in a position of power just as they are.

Don Coviello standing five foot ten, greying hair, silver colored eyes, thick fuzzy eyebrows, tanned skinned, crows feeds under his eyes displaying his seventy two years of a life full of stress and crime.

"That won't be necessary. I came to see if we can come to some type of resolve, understanding even. With that situation involving my granddaughters and the two loves of your life".

Don Coviello said, before pausing giving TK time to take in what he's saying, along with how he knows about his association to them. "Oh you think I've made it in this business, not aware of my surroundings or knowing who the people are that disrespects my family as if I'm not who I am?" He added.

"Being aware is to be alive in this game. But just like the FBI and local police know, who you're looking for isn't here and doesn't plan on coming back. So this is why I don't understand why you wasted time to come here to find this out". TK responded, not liking this old guy's demeanor.

Don Coviello gave off a light laughter, followed by a brief smile, before shifting to a more serious look of business. This is what he really came for.

"This thing of ours. La Costra Nostra, was built on trust respect, loyalty, and honor. Your muli dames disrespected that code. Now there's chatter amongst the other families that me of all people is letting the mulis disrespect La Costra Nostra, which in their eyes is a sign of weakness, since those muli lady friends of yours are still breathing". Don Coviello said with his voice slightly raising to get his point across. TK's face shifting displaying his anger arising, not feeling this old guy's tone or approach, no matter who he is or how old he is. He will get fucked up and put down in here. TK's thinking. Especially with TK's security being the only ones with guns.

"I don't know how you treat people in your house but you will respect me in mine. Now state your business, so I can go on with my day".

The Don's mafia goons looking on at TK wishing they had their weapons, so they could try take him out, setting him straight. They didn't realize TK isn't a regular nigga or muli as the Italians say. He's a gangsta the other gangsters look up to and respect.

"Business as you suggested. This level of disrespect can be forgiven for twenty five percent of what you're bringing in". Don Coviello said knowing TK is in the game.

"You got me fucked up old man!" TK said removing his gold .45 Automatic flipping the safety off, aiming it at the Don, before adding. "I'm a taker, I don't get taken from. Now get the fuck out of my crib, before we bury all you bitch ass mutha fuckas out back!" TK snapped.

Don Coviello being a stone cold killer from the old days, didn't fear the fancy gun staring at him or the tone of TK's voice.

"I'll leave as you wish, but you should know, nothing comes through the ports without my family knowing about it. We run the ports here in Miami, New York and Chicago. I gave you a out. Now you'll see how I became the Don of the most powerful crime family in U. S. History". Don Coviello said eyeing TK with a dark stare wanting to get his point across before turning to exit angered by this cocky ass muli disrespecting him. He's thinking and feeling as he's making his way back to the car. No one has ever disrespected the Don and lived to talk about it.

Between the Don and TK, it's two powerful men, having rank, position and connections in their own respective crime world's. Now they've just clashed like the titans they are. This is not good.

The Fortress Security escorted them to the front gate, giving them their weapons back. At the same time having other security team members on high alert in case these mob goons tried to shoot their way back to the mansion. That would never happen. TK back inside of the mansion, is wishing he would have decided to kill them all right then and there, so he doesn't have any problems with distribution that would create a problem for him back in Mexico. This can't happen, because it's viewed as an obstacle or excuse. As Hector made him aware of Excuses are the demise of all business. Which is not an option.

Chapter 14

9:37 PM Up north, Little Ki Ki, Duttaman, Bundles and Guru, are all at Norma Jeans, in Baltimore, Maryland. They popping bottles, throwing money heavy at the strippers that are exotic and ratchet all at once, shaking their asses, dropping it low, spinning on the pole, spreading their legs wide while hanging upside down on the pole, displaying their strength, skills and the art of their exotic beauty.

Little Ki Ki put this trip together, wanting to show the YG niggas love for always holding her down. She even booked them all suites over at the Renaissance Hotel, overlooking the Harbor. She even bought each of them twenty thousand in Exxon Mobile stocks, so they can always have something to fall back on. Plus for her, this is better than bling. They all respected her position and guidance. Most of which she learned from her con artist ex-girlfriend Karin. Someone she loved and had to put down. That shit hurt her in the worst way, emotionally. Now she's partying in the Charm City, looking to bag another exotic chick, but nothing serious, all fun for the night or a few days, then she'll kick them to the side, with a handbag and good tongue memories to cherish. Little Ki Ki and the team are in VIP attracting all of the attention, with the strippers grinding on them, drinking shots, popping bottles, tossing money and talking heavy. This thick curvaceous tanned white girl with brown hair blond highlights, golden sparkling eyes under the lights. Her body thick like a sista, having the touch of a surgeon, sculpting her to visual perfection.

"Say shawty what they call you?" Little Ki Ki asked, tapping her ass, tucking twenties in her G-string.

"Stage name is Cream, my real name is Amber". She responded with her eyes glowing, adding to her smile with dimples.

"I don't know how they do it up here, but I'm choosing you tonight shawty. You can chase these ones or you can cash out, spending the night with me?" Ki Ki said tapping her ass with the money.

Cream started laughing, turned on by this cute gangsta chick that's balling. Plus she's feeling Little Ki Ki's down south accent. Cream leaned in grinding up on Little Ki Ki, coming closing to her ear. Her lips touching Little Ki Ki's ear, teasing as she started to speak.

"I tried the kissing kitty thing before . It didn't work out as I expected". Cream said.

"You was fucking with the wrong bitch. It's more than the tongue, it's touch". Little Ki Ki responded as her hand slipped across Cream's belly, underneath into her G-string finding her perfectly waxed paradise. Little Ki Ki's fingers finding her spot instantly, sending pleasure through her body, and moans out her mouth, which caught Bundles and Duttaman's attention. They started laughing and trippen, seeing they boss hommie making it happen, doing her thing. Cream's lips up against Little

Ki Ki's ear moaning, lost in the moment. Ki Ki literally having Cream at her finger tips. She stopped, leaving Cream on the sexual edge, wanting to finish, wanting more of this explosive touch, that she's never found even when she's masturbated or used toys. None of the men she dealt with never went straight to her spot like this.

"You can touch me like that for free, as long as you finish next time". Cream responded heated and wet, yearning for more. Duttaman, Bundles and Guru was trying to follow Little Ki Ki's lead, but all the dancers ain't about that life.

The end of the night came, they bounced around to Diamonds, Club Lust, Stage One, The Pussy Cat Club, all before heading back to their suites with women that was down to get the stacks they offering. Back at the suites, they had bottles of Hennessey and blunts followed by sucking and fucking all night.

Ki Ki and Cream made it to the suite overlooking the harbor, where they showered together steaming it up even more, as Ki Ki showed Cream a true lesbian experience, that changed her mind of wanting what's happening to her body to take place all the time.

Little Ki Ki's fingers and tongue massaging, stroking, thrusting, caressing, stimulating Cream's body in every way, creating a powerful surging sensation of orgasms racing through her body. Lost in her touch, she don't even remember exiting the shower, finding their way to the bed, sliding across the sheets, overwhelmed by the intense orgasmic sensations. "Oooh, ooooh, oooh, ooooh, ooooh, I, I, I'm cumming". Cream moaned feeling this uncontrollable wave taking over her body, spraying effortlessly, soaking the sheets, tasting like sweet water to Ki Ki. Little Ki Ki slid off the bed taking ten grand, tossing over the sexy nude Cream.

"You worth it shawty". Little Ki Ki said smiling, feeling herself, position and power. At the same time, savoring Cream's juices over her lips and tongue. Cream is also taking in Little Ki Ki's fit body, she hides under baggie men's clothing.

"You a bad bitch Ki Ki. In bed and looking at your body. If you ever want to dance, these fools would pay top dollar". Cream said, seeing pass the boyish thugged out look. Cream also knowing Ki Ki don't need to dance, it was just a flattering compliment, to let her know she's a bad bitch too.

"This body ain't fo show, only pleasure". Ki Ki responded, as she jump back on the bed climbing up on Cream, allowing her to get a taste of her body, topping her off. Cream also had a magic tongue and fingers, mirroring some of the tricks Ki Ki put on her. "Mmmh, mmmh, damn shawty you good, mmmh, mmmh,". Ki Ki moaned feeling her body coming alive at Cream's tongue and touch. Everything happening is different from Karin's touch. It's new and orgasmic, stirring a welcoming sensation in her body. "Mmmh, mmmh, damn, aaah, aaah". Her moans and breathing intense, her hips gyrating, feeling the orgasm rushing through her body. "Aaaah, aaah, right there shawty, my pussy like your tongue". She let out a pleasure filled moan feeling the intense sensation mounting, stimulating her each time her tongue strategically slid over her clitoris, making her body wet and sensitive. "Damn shawty, aaaah, aaaah,

aaaah". Ki Ki moaned as Cream introduced her fingers into play, thrusting them inside of her tight yet wet pussy. She even placed her finger on Ki Ki's asshole creating a stimulating pressure that turned her on even more, making her moans and breathing pick up just as fast as her gyrating hips. " Aaaah, aaaah, aaaah, mmmmh, damn shawty, aaaah, aaaah". Ki Ki moaned feeling the orgasms taking over her body, racing through her with intense pleasure. Cream can also feel Ki Ki squirting over her tongue and fingers making her go even fast with with her tongue and fingers thrusting in and out, knowing she doing her damn thing. Ki Ki's moans faded to heavy breathing as her orgasms escaped her body rapidly, stimulating her in every way. Cream slowed down allowing Ki Ki to gather herself, before they laid side by side kissing and heavy petting playing with each other's pussy at the same time, lost in each other's touch, wanting to make one another come as much as they possibly could, in between laughing at how good this shit feels, before they fell asleep, drunk off of alcohol and multiple orgasms.

Chapter 15

10:17 AM The next morning, Cream ordered breakfast for her and Little Ki Ki. Scrambled eggs with cheese, bacon, hash browns, wheat toast and cheese grits. For Ki Ki she ordered a crab omelet, fried potatoes, a toasted bagel with cream cheese and fresh squeezed orange juice to chase it all down. Little Ki Ki is sitting up in bed on her cell phone, conducting business as usual. In need of moving the ton TK just dropped on her a couple days ago. A knock came across the room door. Cream got up knowing it's the food she ordered for them. Ki Ki is looking on at Cream's sexy ass body walking away in the nude before taking hold of one of the hotel robes from the mirrored closet on the way to the door. She looked out the peep hole, seeing it is room service. She opened the door greeting him with a smile and her good sex last night glow.

"I have your order, would you like me to set it up for you at the table? He asked, being professional. Cream figured he's working for a bigger tip.

"Yes come on in, that would be nice". She responded, stepping to the side, closing the door behind them. He came over to the table taking the silver caps off of the food, releasing the aroma of all the good food they

103

Part III

ordered. He placed the food in front of the chairs, at the same time glancing over at the nude Little Ki Ki, who's still sitting there on the phone.

"Will you be needing anything else?" He asked. Cream picked that he's now seeking his tip for his service, so she turned heading over to the bed with the money still spread out on it from when Little Ki Ki tossed it in the air showering Cream last night. Cream grabbed a hundred off the bed walking back over to the hotel staff to tip him, only to be greeted with a Glock 9mm staring back at her. He turned her around, pressing the gun to her head, rushing her over to the bed. That's when Little Ki Ki noticed the fast movement, along with the face of the hotel staff. It's Carlos Mendez, the twin brother of Christian Mendez.

He's been watching Little Ki Ki, plotting and patiently awaiting for the moment to catch her slipping, so he can make her pay in blood, for what she did to his brother. Little Ki Ki, seeing him, she moved quick reaching for her .357magnum Red Hawk with hollow point tips, off the night stand. Carlos firing rapid rounds, sending slugs soaring through the air, crashing into Ki Ki's legs, shoulder and back.

"Aaaggh, you bitch ass nigga!!" Little Ki Ki yelled out feeling the pain and heat of the hot slugs eating at her flesh. This still didn't stop her from getting a hold of her Red Hawk pulling the hammer back ready to kill this rat ass nigga, like she should have done before leaving Chicago.

Carlos is using Cream as a shield, closing in on where he seen Little Ki Ki go down after she fell off the bed. She seen his tactic in using Cream, so she fired off three thunderous rounds from the Red Hawk, each slug going through Cream's body into Carlos thrusting both of their bodies back with brute force. Cream died before she hit the floor, no love loss for Ki Ki, she's in survivor beast mode. As for Carlos, he was hit in the chest and stomach. Now he's in fear of being killed by this bitch that is responsible for killing his brother. He couldn't die like this without getting revenge, he's thinking.

"Es muy tarde pendeja! You going to die today, for killing mi hermano!" Carlos shouted out in anger, letting Ki Ki know it's too late. Carlos is holding his stomach feeling the pain of the bullets that entered his stomach. He can feel something is wrong with his body, he can't die like this without getting revenge. He's thinking and feeling. Carlos came around to the side of the bed where Ki Ki started shooting from.

Immediately, he seen a trail of blood leading under the bed. At the same time, he heard her voice coming from the other side of the room.

"Like your brother, you rat ass niggas need to die!" She said after she pulled herself to the other side of the bed.

She squeezed the trigger unleashing the remaining deadly hollow point slugs, slamming into his chest, thrusting his body back. Each brute slug tearing a fist size hole in his torso. He could feel his life leaving his flesh as he crashed down on the floor, taking His last breath in fear of this very moment. Little Ki Ki badly injured, hurrying grabbing her phone, sneakers and a robe, knowing she needs to get to a hospital now. She looked down at

105

Cream, "Sorry for that shawty". She said making her way to the door, opening it, seeing Bundles, Duttaman, and Guru running down the long hall towards her room with their guns out at the ready, having heard the gunshots. A hotel maid that's in the hall came up to Little Ki Ki.

"Are you okay?" She asked.

Little Ki Ki turned towards the female's voice with that Chicago accent. Soon as she locked eyes with the female, the Latina thrust a razor sharp knife into Little Ki Ki's heart with force, anger and revenge.

"You fucked with the wrong family!" The Latina said abruptly turning the knife, sealing Little Ki Ki's fate for sure. Then she snatched the knife out just as as hard and fast as she slammed it in. Her eyes still locked on Ki Ki watching her suck in and exhale her last breath. Ki Ki's body dropping to the floor in what seemed like slow motion to Bundles and them in disbelief that this is happening to their thugged out hommie, the realest gangsta bitch in the game.

Duttaman aiming his twin, black steel snub nose .44 magnums at the Latina, dumping, squeezing off thunderous rounds that roared and raced through the air crashing violently into her flesh, almost severing her left arm from her body, as the slugs forced her body up against the wall, she slid down lifeless, unable to survive the onslaught of slugs. The Latina was Catrina, the sister of the twins.

"Yo let's get the fuck out of here!" Guru said, not wanting to get caught.

"Damn Ki Ki see you on the other side in a gangsta's paradise". Bundles said.

106

Bundles gave a brief pause looking on at Little Ki Ki, honoring her true G, knowing she was the realest bitch he and his team ever met. She showed them love and the game on many levels, legal and illegal. Wanting them to see there is a endgame and out. Not the one she has faced today. Bundles brief moment was interrupted when he heard doors wing opened followed by police radios squawking.

"Let's go nigga". Duttaman shouted pulling on Bundles arm. They took off running fast towards the staircase, not wanting to take the elevator, wanting to evade police questions, contact and a shootout with the law, because they wasn't about to go back to jail. They would rather die in the free world before they died in a cell shackled and cuffed. They leaped down flights of steps, coming down to the first floor when a hotel security popped into the stairs seeing them. The security attempting to stop them removing his gun until Guru, Duttaman and Bundles all removed their guns aiming at him. Seeing this level of danger and his shift and life ending right here, he dropped his weapon, pleading for his life.

"Go ahead man, I don't want to die". The security said closing his eyes not even wanting to remember these goons he know would not hesitate to kill him. They made their escape never looking back to the guard or this city that claimed the life of their big hommie Ki Ki.

Chapter 16

Within a few hours of the shootout at the Renaissance Hotel, the news outlets were all over it. Making the connection of Carlos Mendez to his twin, that was also a known king pin and nephews of cartel Boss Roberto Romero, from Tijuana, Mexico. The FBI also catching wind of this shootout that halted their continuous investigation into Little Ki Ki, TK, Red Rain, Suga Baby and the Mendez twins for their previous arrest, sudden release or escape from custody, also the large cocaine distribution. Little Ki Ki leaving behind millions in cash, Bitcoin, Doge coin, along with a ton of cocaine she has stashed away at one of her properties.

TK is at home when alerts came through on his phone, making him tune into the news on his sixty inch flat screen TV, seeing the looped footage of the graphic crime scene, that left the little hommie dead. This shit didn't sit right with him, making him grit his teeth, clenching his jaw wanting to avenge Ki Ki, but the work was already done. Now the cops are trying to figure who offed the female that dealt the death penalty for Little Ki Ki, with the sharp knife.

A loss like this is not good for TK, having his little hommie taken out hurts emotionally. Losing the ton he fronted her, hurts financially. That's money that he'll have to compensate for without any excuses being forwarded to Hector back in Mexico. All of this shit happening without his ride or die bitches Red Rain and Suga Baby, to help him bounce back and keep this shit under control. For him, his world as he's known it for a couple years, is starting to fall apart. TK tried to call the only other people he trust, to pull his family back together. All to no avail. Neither Suga Baby or Red Rain answered their phones, which is angering him even more. The feeling of not having control over the business or the women in his life. He sat the phone down to pour himself a much needed double shot of Hennessey XO to take the edge and stress off of losing Ki Ki and the ton.

Without question he's still going to hold Little Ki Ki down, having her body brought to Atlanta, paying for her funeral. Making sure the hood she was raised in and showed her love, will get their chance to pay their respects. He also has to get word to Trappa-D that he ain't got to worry about nothing as long as he's out here. TK figured Little Ki Ki was holding him down, and she still is, even in death. She had real life insurance, making Trappa-D the sole benefactor. It was Karin and Trappa-D, but after Karin tried that bullshit Little Ki Ki took her off of it.

What TK isn't seeing, is the blessing in every bad situation. With the Mendez twins gone, he has full control and reign over the Midwest and East coast. He just have to put a new team in place to fill those positions. So many thoughts running through his head as he's pouring another double shot, at the same time his cell phone sounding off. He glanced over at it, not in a hurry to answer with all that's going on right now. He downed his double shot, before answering the phone.

"I'll be there to get what belongs to me Agent Kemp, so tell that piece of shit, he can't stop me". TK said before hanging up, taking hold of his other cell phone to look up CBP Agent Marlon Kemp. He found info on Facebook, Instagram and (X) Twitter. Him, his wife, kids, friends and family.

"You fucked up Marlon". TK said seeing this info on this crooked agent. He tracked his home address using Google map, seeing a overview of his home.

TK moving fast to secure Marlon's family, using them to exchange for the product that Hector fronted him, which is ten tons of uncut raw grade A cocaine. Within a couple of hours TK had Marlon's townhouse secured. His wife and children bound at the feet, hands, with their mouths duct tape close.

"Trisha, your husband thinks he can play games with my product that is way more valuable to me than you and your two children". TK said. She started crying realizing how dangerous this man is, having no respect for her or her children's lives. TK having her cell phone in hand added. " I'm going to call him, when he see first hand. I'm not bluffing, you'll be able to see how much he loves and values you and your children". He tapped the screen calling up the preset Hubby, calling up Marlon, who answered on the second ring seeing it's a incoming call from his wife.

"Hey honey buns". Agent Kemp answered. TK gave a brief smile knowing he has this scumbag.

111

"You a soft ass mutha fucka. Your honey buns is in a bad position because of that stupid shit you trying to pull".

"You can't do this, I'm a federal agent". He blurted through the phone, attempting to use his cop card, all too late.

"That shit went out of the door, the moment you decided to fuck with my product. I have people at the ports. I want you to sign off, releasing my shipping containers. My drivers will take it from there".

"I'll do it, just don't hurt my family". He responded sounding panicked. He did as instructed. It's done, your men should be picking it up now".

TK looking at his phone seeing a text just came through, acknowledging the release of the containers. "I should put a bullet in your wife's face for you wasting my time. If you or them Italian mutha fuckas try that shit again, I'm a kill each one of y'all in front of your families". TK said tossing the phone over by Trisha as he exited the home feeling back in power.

A hour later, the drivers reached the warehouse previously owned by La Vieja. TK is also present to set eyes on the product as he always do, before directing each to their destination. The only difference now, he has no one to direct it all to. When the containers popped open, nothing is as it normally would be. Each container is empty.

"Did y'all grab the right containers?!" TK snapped. The drivers showing him the papers that match the identification numbers on the containers. The plastic seals weren't even broken. They couldn't have come like this. The mafia or the CBP agent must have put new seals on the containers. TK called the ports wanting to speak with Agent Kemp.

"Agent Kemp there?"

"He took off sick". TK hung up pissed off all over again. " Lets go get this mutha fucka". TK said to his security, then added directing the drivers. "You two head back to the ports and find my shit!" Once inside of the jet black Rolls Royce truck, his driver took him back to the Kemp residents. It didn't take long, before they raced up to the townhouse steps, kicking in the front door, guns out at the ready to kill Marlon and his family. TK Raced upstairs ready to gun down this piece of shit.

Nothing. No one, the house is empty.

"I knew I should've killed them mutha fuckas!" TK snapped. He was duped by this crooked agent and the mafia, taking his product. Marlon having been a cop out LA he new high ranking gang members that would by this product, giving him enough money to flee the country. TK is going to track Marlon, using his resources, then kill him and all he loves right where he stands.

Chapter 17

Within twenty four hours of being deceived, TK along with his Fortress security team headed out to the west coast, having found Agent Marlon Kemp at a motel in a small town outside of Albuquerque. A motel on a main highway that Marlon figure he could hide safely with his wife and children, until he was able to find a buyer for the product he stole from TK. Marlon made contact with old associates who's planning to meet with him in person, to go over the numbers and logistics of when and where to pick up the product. TK having his security approach the motel door, with them looking very professional, dressed in suits posing as FBI agents. The presence and first impression, will make Marlon lower his guard, thinking he's amongst friendlies. They knocked on the door, standing firm awaiting him to answer, at the same time prepared for any contingent plans he may have outside of going with what they have in store for him.

Inside of the room, Marlon became alert, thinking it's his California contact. He made sure his wife tended to the kids sitting them in front of the TV watching cartoons. Marlon came to the door, looking through the peep hole, seeing two suits. He opened the door greeting them.

"How's it going guys". Marlon said trying to be professional, while holding his gun in his hand behind the door. "I'm Federal Agent Schmidt, this is Agent Stony, we would like to speak to you, Marlon Kemp, a CBP Agent in regards to a shipment of government hard drives that were differed to you".

"What? That doesn't even make sense. I don't need any hard drives". Marlon said. Marlon standing five nine, thick built, weighing a solid two hundred pounds, a close beard looking a little rough, flowing with his small uncombed afro.

The trained Fortress security not even giving him time to really assess what's going on, they moved fast pressing their guns in his face, as they pushed into the room, they took his gun from him, before securing him and his family, then called the others, along with TK, who entered the room pissed off, unable to sleep, full of anger that's visible in his murderous eyes that's staring down Marlon wanting to give him a beat down then torture him and his family, just for trying to mind fuck him and steal his product. TK also knowing he couldn't afford to take a loss of this amount. Even if he could, he wants about to bow down to this crooked agent.

"I want my product, no games, or I will cut those kids up one one by in front of you and your wife, until you see them take their last breath in fear of what's happening to them".

"You're going to kill us all no matter what. I know how this works". Marlon fired back, not caring about his wife and kids or attempting to try to save them, so they don't have to pay for his greed and crooked behavior. His

116

wife is oblivious to it all, yet loving her husband enough to flee, with being in danger the first time.

"Marlon without question you're a dead, you can't save yourself. You can save those two innocent children and Honeybun's as you call your beautiful wife who is looking confused and terrified right now". TK said still staring at Marlon ready to get this over, introducing his face to a full clip. Marlon now thinking how he fucked up having his family trail along with him, placing them in immanent danger. All he wanted to do is have unlimited cash flow to give his wife the world, especially with working check to check struggling with rising gas prices and inflation. Marlon looking over at his wife and kids, who are visibly shaken.

"I'm sorry for this, I wanted a better life for us". Marlon said.

"I love you babe, please don't let them hurt me or the children". She pleaded also having heard the option TK has given her husband to save her and the kids.

"Not here, don't kill me here. I'll tell you where the product is". Marlon said.

"Your family will stay with us until we get the product. Then and only then we'll let them go". TK responded.

TK's men rounded the Marlon's wife and kids up, taking them to another location, he felt comfortable with, especially not knowing who Marlon told to meet him at his motel. He didn't want to be here when they showed up, under the pretense that they would be buying the product Marlon stole from him. Then he and his team would have to dispose of them too. Marlon gave

117

TK the location to the product. TK and his team flew back to the east coast, where Marlon took them to get the product that was in a storage unit he rented. Once inside of the unit TK made sure all of his product was there having his team along with Marlon load it on the big rig truck that came to secure it.

"Step back into the storage you stupid nigga". TK directed Marlon as he removed his custom gold .45 automatic.

"Can, can you at least make it so someone can find me in here. I want a decent funeral and if you leave me here I'll decompose. This unit is paid for six months under a bogus name. Marlon pleaded not wanting his body to rot, where his family couldn't have a proper funeral, unable to recognize him.

"That's not my worry. You should have thought about dying gracefully before you fucked with my product". TK said, firing off two rounds to the head and body killing him instantly, forcing his body back into the storage unit that will be his grave until he's discovered.

TK now feeling better about getting his product back also checking this bitch ass fed that tried to play him. As for Marlon's family, he couldn't let them go, risking a chance for them to tell about him being linked to killing Marlon, so he gave his team the go ahead to make them all disappear, no trace. They did just that killing the entire family, burying them in the Nevada desert. Even if somehow their bodies did resurface the vultures and other animals will feed off their flesh, vanishing all traces of their existence.

Chapter 18

Within three weeks of sending Don Coviello the dead Agent Marlon Kemp's bloody badge. Many attempts on TK's life has been made from the mafia and it's Italian associates looking to make their bones. All attempts failed, having the best trained security in the world, they never even came close. TK's mansion now having additional Fortress Security members with this threat becoming more of a problem. This is also why TK green lighted the Fortress Security's trained team to take out Don Carmine Coviello. In doing so it would be worth a million for their off the book services. They didn't hesitate to take up the offer, having had their men shot at by mob figures in attempt to get to TK.

The Fortress Security team making their way to Long Island, where Don Coviello resided in a ten thousand square foot mansion looking like a miniature White House. Each member moving under the cover of night. For them it's just like the old days in the military on special ops missions. Don Coviello comfortable in his position of power not having trained security like TK, only mafia gangsters the normal citizen would fear, not these elite soldiers. They noticed two men standing out in front of the mansion talking and smoking cigarettes.

They didn't even see the Fortress Team coming, silenced rounds dropping them in mid conversation, never giving them a chance to alert those inside. They moved quick entering the home, coming in contact with two more mafia goons sitting in the living room counting money. Soon as they seen the fast movement of the Fortress security, their attempts to reach for the guns on the coffee table, was halted by silenced rounds crashing into their heads, clearing all thoughts of getting a shot off. They swept the downstairs area clearing it, before moving to the second floor, proceeding to the closed master bedroom door. It's locked, the lead member noticed, signalling to the others behind him that he's about to breach the door with his foot.

He counted down using his fingers, showing three, two, one. Then it happened. His foot thrusting into the door, each of them fanning out surrounding the large bed where the Don is sitting up reading while his wife is watching television. The look in Don Coviello's eyes are murderous not liking that these men made it into his home pass his men, as if they don't know or respect him or his position of power. The murderous look he's giving them trying to stare through their mask, as if he's still in control. His reign ends right here and now.

"I don't know who you men are, but you kill me, there will be a war until my family finds who is responsible!" Don Coviello stated firmly.

The trained men didn't say a word, only firing off silenced center mass shots, on him and his wife who tried to scream with no luck. Slugs finding her open mouth too, making it look like a sanctioned Mafia hit. Each of their bodies slumped in bed lifeless.

Don Coviello was right, once his body is discovered, the underboss of the family will immediately point the finger at the other four families in New York, not realizing the Don underestimated the position of power TK possesses, all because he views him as a nigger or as the Italians say Muli. Unlike the mafia, TK didn't need permission to kill a made man, a Mafia Don.

The moment Don Coviello sent men attempting to take him out, it opened the door costing the lives of those protecting him, including his wife. While the Fortress's security made their exit, to head back to Florida, on the other side of the country in California three hours behind the east coast time, the FBI having received tips of Suga Baby and Red Rain's whereabouts in Compton, hidden amongst the Bloods. Someone outside of the hood catching wind of these two boss bitches buying heavy work, flooding the hood. Both women only knowing how to hustle getting to this paper while staying low supplying the hood allowing every body a chance to eat. At the same time giving the Five Star Blood his cut, for protecting them and giving them a place to stay.

"One time! One time!" The look outs yelled seeing the unmarked Crown Vics coming through, along with uniformed police officer's squad cars, coming a dozen deep. The look outs also alerting the hood bosses through text, unmarked cars are coming along with LAPD with the ghetto bird in the air. The FBI being informed by the LAPD that coming into this hood unnoticed would be hard to do. Everyone here knows all the faces of the people who belongs in this hood. No new fiends or friends. This is Blood controlled turf, nothing less.

Two helicopters hovering above the hood. One chopper is FBI, the other is LAPD. The dozen cars came to a halt, then all the agents and officers seeming to exit in synch. Agents Douglas and Smalls are also present taking lead since they loss the tail in South Dakota. They didn't want to make the same mistake. One of the LAPD plain clothes detectives came up to the agents.

"These fools out here are going to try to play hard ball, go just as hard to show these gang banging mutha fuckas we came to make arrest. Now follow me. I know which one to talk to". Detective Gibson said.

He's a dark skinned brother with a bald head, thick eyebrows, clean shaven face, looking serious like he could be a gang member. If it wasn't to for law enforcement he may have been in a gang, especially being raised in this hood, until he found his way out.

Detective Gibson walked over to the house with the most Bloods standing around. Normally they would all be strapped having their weapons in plain sight, in case a drive by was going down or if they had someone trying to jack one of the hommies. Once they was alerted to the police presents, they hid or tucked their weapons. "What up blood?" The big hommie said.

"Agents Douglas and Smalls have body warrants for two fine ass sistas. I mean they some bad bitches, physically and literally. Word got back to them that these sexy beast, is held up in ya hood doing numbers". Detective Gibson said to the six foot two, muscle bound Blood with tattoos of chains on both of his massive biceps. Big

Bolo, did fifteen years for slinging guns, and shooting rival gang members.

"Yo blood you got bad Intel from the rat nigga that told you that stupid shit". Big Bolo responded.

"Look around mutha fucka! There's a dozen units and two ghetto birds in the sky. You think we move on bad Intel? Them bitches is up in this hood and we ain't leaving until we get them. So you want to protect them, they must be paying you good. It better be worth it, because we find them you going to jail nigga, and you know that'll be ya third strike". Detective Gibson snapped trying to get resolve. He turned to Agents Douglas and Smalls. "We can start here searching his house". He added. Agent Douglas also agreeing knowing they have to search all of the blood related houses, as reported to them from their CIs. With the bounty of five hundred thousand on these women, the CIs and rats are coming out to hopefully collect.

"You want to search my crib y'all need a warrant". Big Bolo said.

"These men have body warrants and the belief their suspects are inside. They don't give a fuck about ya guns or drugs. This is bigger than you". Detective Gibson said leading the way into the house removing his side arm. The agents following suit, not knowing what to expect, guns out in front sweeping through each room. Beer bottles on the table, a scale visible on the kitchen counter, AK-47 in the closet they searched, making sure no one is hiding inside. Money under the bed and in bags on the floor. The FBI agents now preparing to leave when Agent Douglas noticed a Gucci diaper bag, just like the one

Suga Baby had at the airport. He rushed over searching its contents: Diapers, wipes, baby powder, lotion, along with four ten grand stacks of hundred dollar bills at the bottom of the diaper bag. Agent Douglas seeing this can't take the money, since his warrant is solely a body warrant for the two suspects. He will question to find out who the owner of this diaper bag is because it is too much of a coincidence that his CIs told him these women are here, and now this same Gucci diaper bag is here, but they're not. They made their way back downstairs out to the front of the house where Big Bolo stood with his gang talking and secretly giving directions.

"Big man, you got a baby?" Agent Douglas questioned. Big Bolo looking at the diaper bag in his hand, already knowing which direction he's going.

"I got babies, what do you expect after being locked down for so long, now I'm busting up in every bitch I smash". Big Bolo responded humoring himself and his goons.

Big Bolo received a text from Suga Baby about forgetting her son's diaper bag when she hurried out of the house to evade the fast approaching feds and cops. Right now her and Red Rain are at another of the Blood connected house that doesn't have members around it, which made the cops stop in front of this crib. Agent Douglas dropped the diaper bag walking up to Big Bolo.

"We're going to find them, or keep coming back until we do. You'll either get tired of us showing up, or tired of protecting them, when you start losing money and men for all the guns and drugs we see".

124

"Do you fool, and I'm a hold it down on this end, no matter what y'all pigs try to throw at us". Big Bolo said. The agents continued searching the area and other gang protected homes. Only to come up empty handed. No sight of these two women. This angered both of the federal agents even more, feeling like they are close, yet the slipped away again, making them look like the fools, especially with them having the advantage of this unexpected raid, thanks to their CIs, and they still failed. In the mean time the two underground queens Suga Baby and Red Rain will continue building their empire, getting even more love respect from the Bloods, while making this money.

Chapter 19

Over the last three weeks, TK is feeling the pressure of having to move this product, minus Little Ki Ki, Red Rain and Suga Baby. Being in survival business mode, he was networking up and down the coast, linking up with the Harrisburg YGs, North Carolina's Trent 'T-Geez' Graves, a project nigga about his paper and women, since he thinks he's a real pimp.

TK also headed back to Atlanta where he found Little Dre, that's from Trappa-D and Little Ki Ki's hood. He like the rest of this hood are all rocking R. I. P. Little Ki Ki t-shirts, along with FREE Trappa-D, on the other shirts and baseball caps. It was only right TK blessed them, making Little Dre responsible. TK also linked up with Tre-Breezy from York, Pennsylvania, no relation to his Crip hommie Tre from Pittsburgh. He also reached out to him, spreading the love, putting him in position.

Now having connected with all of the players, he needed to move the tons of cocaine Hector keeps sending, expecting his millions in return. Hector didn't care about Little Ki Ki or Red Rain and Suga Baby not being around to move the product. In his eyes, using them as a excuse to not get his money, is a problem, so TK never made it an issue or a topic. He just produced the money for the product as it came in. TK did recouped the money he loss on the ton he fronted Little Ki Ki. He still wanting to track down where she kept it, because at the end of the day, that shit still belongs to him. TK even suggested to the YG niggas if they came up on it, he would bless them with half of it. For him getting it back would be a plus, so splitting fifty fifty wouldn't be problem. It also became incentive for the YG niggas to put full effort into finding it. Little Ki Ki had that shit put up secured always having layers between herself and the product. TK now having figured out one problem, while another is arising, him not realizing the hit he put on Don Coviello, would not just start a war amongst the families.

He would also feel the wrath at the ports, with the Coviello attacking any and all that had beef with the family. The dead Agent Kemp who was on Don Coviello's payroll also creating questioning with his absence from work. His coworkers even going to his home, along with making attempts to connect with his wife, who's family is also worried about her and the children's whereabouts.

Both the federal agent and the Mafia Don allowed their greed to get the best of them. Now with all of this unfolding, made Mafia goons vowing to whack TK knowing he has had a hand in the deaths of the Don and the agent on the family's payroll. First, they're going to take any and all product coming into the ports, registered to the companies that are still under La Vieja's name, that he controls, via her legal business associates and sons who are the benefactors to her legal and illegal millions that didn't belong to Cartel Boss Hector. The cocaine came through the Miami Ports, just as the vacuum sealed bails of money he shipped back to Mexico to one of Hector's companies. TK is on his way back to Miami traveling in a convoy of three Stealth grey G55 AMG Mercedes Benz trucks, tinted out, equipped with armor to protect their client. These vehicles owned and operated by Fortress Elite Security. This next level security is why TK pays them well, including monthly bonuses for extracurricular details. A call came through on TK's Kryptail cell phone, which is only for direct business with Hector, Armando or Salvator. So when it rings he sets all conversation and personal play to the side.

"What's good amigo?" TK answered.

"Yo no se hermano. This is why I call you". Armando said, making TK wonder what's wrong since, he got the last shipment, moved the product and sent the money back.

"Everything is on schedule last I checked". TK said assuring Armando his timing with business is always on point. The money was sent back to Mexico a week ago. The new shipment should be on it's way today as scheduled.

"You can imagine Hermano, we go to secure the dinero, pero, es nada". Armando said making him aware there was no money. This hit TK hard, knowing this amount of money he cannot replace ten million cash with ease. If it was a loss he had to take, he would be pissed, gunning for whoever fucked with his money. But having ten million of Hector's money come up missing, is a big problem and not a good look for TK. He can feel his blood boiling as thoughts of having to face Hector, of the reality of taking a loss. He would have to sell everything to stay on the pay schedule.

"One second Armando, let me call my new guy at the ports on my other phone". TK said assessing the number calling up his guy with the CBP.

"Agent Schmidt speaking, how can I help you?"

"Keith it's me TK. Is everything good down there?"

"Yes sir, as far as my eyes can see".

"I need you to look closer for container number 05839304. That was sent out a week ago". TK stated sounding irritated and rightfully so.

A few seconds after he punched in on the computer, it came up.

"I'm showing that container was routed to New York to a Frank Coviello".

"How the fuck was it rerouted without me knowing!? Who's responsible for this!?" TK snapped, now knowing his money was stolen. His blood is boiling ready to kill Frank Coviello and all connected to rerouting his money.

"Sir there was another shipment that was due today, it's showing it too has been rerouted". Agent Schmidt said.

TK can feel the weight dropping on him all at once. This crushing feeling can only be resolved by bodies dropping, blood being spilled even if he gets it all back, they have to pay for disrespecting his gangsta. TK not realizing Don Coviello's death only made matters worst. Now he has to kill them all off, if he wants to prevail from these multimillion dollar interceptions, that could cost him his position and life.

130

"Armando I located the money, I'll have it resent". TK said, angered by what's unfolding.

"I'll contact you in a few days hermano, no excuses". Armando said ending the call. Armando having heard the tone of TK's voice snapping on the CBP Agent so he is now aware of this problem with their millions that should be in Mexico.

After the call, Armando relayed this delay to Hector who wasn't fond of hearing excuses no matter who they came from, even if TK has made him even more money than La Vieja with his expansion on the East coast and Midwest. TK was always early or on time with all payments, so this new occurrence, doesn't describe the person Hector is hearing about right now. He knows TK isn't trying to get over on him, plus La Vieja vouched for him which means a lot. This is also the reason he's not sending a dozen assassins to take him and all he loves out.

"Armando, go to the States to see if the Hermano needs our assistance". Hector said, standing on the side of the pool table with the stick in his hand taking a shot making a break to start a new game. "Whoever rerouted that money also stole from me, so make an example out of them". Hector added.

Armando now exiting to fulfill his cartel duties gangland style. Hector looking over at Salvator standing on the other side of the pool table with his stick.

"Sal, I want you to find the two women and the baby TK values and bring them here". Hector said, thinking ahead, knowing leverage is always key when it comes to his money and staying on top in this business.

"I've been keeping an eye on them anyway, since they managed to slip from the FBI, making their way to California". Sal said, knowing this whole thing that's taking place is all because if these two broads. Salvator is also aware of the FBI attempting to find them in Compton amidst the Bloods, with no luck. This only means he has to use his special resources to make sure they're in and out, to get these women and child to Mexico, as leverage or disposal depending how Hector is feeling, if his money isn't produced.

Chapter 20

Within forty eight hours TK is making calls to his gang affiliated hommies up north. The Harrisburg YGs, Pittsburgh Crips ran by the hommie Tre and Wheezy. Tre reached out to the City of Gods that's Cripping in New York. They had their ear to the streets hearing about a lot of product is about to land, that's going to drop the prices, plus it's grade A shit.

TK put the Mafia Capo's name out there to the New York Crips who found out where this goomba hangs at. TK hearing about the location, so he wanted to be present so he got ready to leave his Miami mansion to fly up to New York. Soon as he opened the front door, he's greeted by Armando. At first he thought the sight of him unexpectedly meant death. In most cases it would be. He was also wondering why his team didn't alert him to a guest being present. TK's left hand reaching towards his waistline.

"Tranquillo hermano. If I or Hector wanted you dead, you would never have a chance to reach for a weapon. Hector sent me to see if I can help with this financial delay". Armando said.

"I'm on my way to New York to come face to face with the person I believe is responsible". TK responded.

"Who is this person you speak of?"

"Mafia Capo, Frank Coviello". TK said before giving him a quick run down on all that went down, including the origin of it all.

"I have a jet on standby at our disposal". Armando said.

"I already have a private jet booked, I'll meet you up there". He responded heading out to the private airport focused on getting the tons of cocaine and the ten million dollars back. Armando also offended by this Mafia Capo doing as he wish stealing the tons shipped by Hector, then the millions due to Hector as payment, so they feel as if he's disrespecting them too. As they're in route to New York, over on the West Coast in Compton, Salvator's contracted associates are already in motion, in pursuit of Suga Baby and Red Rain. The hood where Red Rain and Suga Baby are hiding up at, four custom designed drones outfitted with infrared cameras, along with firing capabilities from a 9mm based mechanism, designed specifically for these covert drones, that are manned by off site contractors.

"Targets located". The Off site contractor said, keeping one drone hovering high over the house Red Rain and Suga Baby is in. The other three drones spreading out in the hood, preparing to have multiple angles, covering the entrance and exit of the team sent to get the ladies and child out.

Three all black Chevy Suburbans with tinted windows concealing all inside rolled into the hood. All of the look outs chirping and sounding off, making everyone alert. At the same time, they noticed the drones hovering too, so they started taking aim shooting at the drones, until the Off site contractor remotely fired on Blood gang members below dropping them with head and body shots, while forcing the other gang members to take cover, clearly seeing they're at a disadvantage with this technology. The drones closed in on the house monitoring all exits and windows as six men exited the Suburbans in stealth grey fatigues, matching warpaint on their faces, silenced weapons at the ready, as they moved with trained precision executing the mission at hand, dropping those in front with tranquilizer darts, as they rushed up the steps into the house dropping all inside that isn't their targets.

"Second floor two adults and a child". The Off site contractor relayed to the team through their ear pieces. They closed in on the second floor ready for contact, already knowing these two women can and will be violent if need be. Suga Baby and Red Rain didn't have a chance to flee as before, which is why they got stuck on the second floor. They moved quick closing in on the bedroom with the door open, no one in sight, yet the real time intelligence is telling them the occupants are inside. " Caution, both adults are now up against the wall looking to embrace for contact". The Off site contractor said.

Right then, they removed their live weapons with real bullets, with this threat of combatants in the room. Then they lead operative tossed a flash bang into the room. Soon as it erupted, it shook both of the women who didn't expect it, causing them to drop their weapons. The roaring of the flash bang also startled TK junior, making him cry out in fear.

"Don't throw anymore! We have a baby in here!" Suga Baby yelled out, unable to see due to the brightness of the flash bang, coupled with the smoke. Her nor Red Rain realized the trained operatives are standing a few feet away from them with their guns aimed at them. At the same time the Off site contractor is relaying to them.

"A call just went into the 911 dispatch of shots being fired, get out of there. The closest police unit is less than three minutes away".

They moved quick, firing tranquilizer rounds in each female to avoid further resistance. Then they removed both of them and the child, making their exit just as smooth as they entered until a gang members yelled out. "Let them go before we wet y'all up!"

Suddenly men from the other Suburbans exiting, firing rapid darts on the big mouth gang members dropping them. The drones also lowered to protect the operatives, taking aim at the approaching gang members. The operatives all made it into the trucks safely, along with targets they came for. The convoy took off just as fast as they came, all followed by the drones assisting a smooth exit. Then the drones shot to three hundred feet in the air in a matter of seconds, following the convoy from a far, keeping a eye on the package as they're paid to do. Suga Baby and Red Rain by the time they awake they'll be in Mexico amongst the world's most notorious violent underground crime figure. He will use them in exchange for his money or product if need be. Even then, he still may kill them off just to prove a point of, don't fuck with his money, power or business.

Chapter 21

Bronx, New York 7:04 PM Eastern time. The hommie Tre and Wheezy along with Sheff Da Hommie and Sleepy Cuz, two thugged out New York Crip niggas, that's been getting money in the hood. They all linked up before entering Coviello's Fine Italian Cuisine, owned by the Coviello Crime Family. It's also known to be frequented by mob associates.

Sleepy Cuz standing six foot one, medium built, always high and ready to put that work in. Dark skinned, clean shaven face, thick eyebrows, enhancing his dark stare and red eyes from being high. Sheff Da Hommie having dreadlocks to the shoulder, a brown skin Crip nigga with platinum fronts. Standing a husky five foot seven, always on go, keeping his .45 automatic with extended clip at the ready. The head Crips entered with a dozen street soldiers, all of the customers are looking on intently pointing at the serious looking goons dressed in majority blue and black, with guns visible on their waistlines and in their hands.

"Excuse me! Excuse me, you can't be in here without reservations". The staff member said, lying, not wanting their kind in this nice establishment, dressed as they are. Tre displaying his modified .40mm with a extended clip.

"This is my reservation! Now where the fuck is that nigga Frank Coviello at cuz!?" Tre aggressively said, getting his point across.

"He's in the back". The staff quickly said pointing towards the back of the restaurant.

"Tell that piece of shit we have a order to put in!" Sleepy Cuz said eyeing the staff down, ready to start shooting. Before the employee could respond, Frank came from the back, exiting with five Mafia goons.

"You frign muli gang bangers come up into my place being disrespectful like you don't know what's good for you!" Frank snapped removing his nickel plated .357 snub nose. His goons also removing their weapons too, which set off a chain reaction of the heavily armed Crips, all taking aim at Frank.

"Yo cuz you don't want that type of party up in here.
We live this gang shit to the fullest cuz! We will splash all you mutha fuckas up in here cuz!" Tre asserted firmly. The Crip hommies moving in spreading out, guns locked on Frank, giving him and his Mafia comrades a visual of how this shit is about to play out. Frank never having this amount of disrespect imposed on him. He's usually the one doing killing and disrespecting.

"Okay, okay, state ya business, so you and your frign hoodlum friends can get the fuck out of my place already!" Frank stated with aggression and resentment of their presence.

Frank a forty nine year old Mafia Capo, standing five foot eight, thick build from lifting and eating good Italian food. Black hair combed back, dark colored eyes, thick eyebrows, allowing his murderous look to be taken serious, when he's staring at those who crossed him or the family.

"We here for the money and product you stole from da hommie cuz. It belongs to a friend of ours as your Italian mutha fuckas say". Sheff Da Hommie said, with his finger inside of trigger guard, ready to down this fake ass John Gotti nigga. Frank started laughing while looking back and forth to his goombas. Sleepy Cuz fired a round into the face of Frank's Mafia associates halting his laughter, ejecting chunks of his skull and brains out of the other side of his head. Making a ten million dollar, ten ton statement, showing these Mob figures how serious they are.

"Ya boy right there was a casualty you could have prevented. Now shake that money and product loose cuz". Tre said. Before Frank could respond, a call came through on his cell phone. Frank can hear it ringing, yet choosing to ignore it, in case these crazy Crip thugs think he's going for another weapon. They would gun him down without hesitation.

"Answer that shit cuz so you can see how real this shit is". Sheff Da Hommie said, already knowing it's a call coming from the big cuz that hired them. It's TK reaching out to Frank via his daughter Victoria's cell phone.

Since him and Armando snatched up her and Priscilla. For ten million cash, and ten tons of uncut cocaine. The entire Coviello Family's life is on the line. Soon as Frank answered the phone's Face Time, he can see a bound and distraught Victoria and Priscilla. No matter how hard of a mobster he is. A made man's weakness is his daughter or daughters because they would give them the world, at the same time destroy it to protect them. Frank can see the fear in their eyes, wanting to live and be set free from this very moment, that's terrifying. Frank never expected to be made as the one who high-jacked TK for his money and product. Nor did he think his daughters would be caught up in his mob lifestyle.

"You frign lay a hand on them, you won't see dime I tell ya!" Frank said as the video shift, showing a very pissed off TK.

"Where's my money and product?" TK asked with his gun to Victoria's temple, displaying his level of seriousness.

"The product never left Miami, even though it looks like it. I didn't want to risk moving that much product coming into the New York Ports even if we run them. I reverted it back in the computer this morning". Frank said, being satisfied with the money, at the same time, he would have taken the product once he figured out the logistics of distribution. TK hearing what he said so he called his guy at the Miami Ports.

"Agent Schmidt here".

"Keith run those numbers to my container, tell me if it's there". He did as instructed, coming back over the phone with good news.

"Yes sir it's here, which is fast, how did that happen?" Agent Schmidt asked thinking the product went to New York and back.

"Don't worry about that, make sure it stays there and never leave your sight".

"I'm on it right now". He said hanging.

"So far your word has saved one of your daughters. What about my ten million?"

"It's not ten, but I can get you at least seven of it". He responded, having gave the underboss his cut, his crew got their cut, he kept the rest.

Armando came into the view of the camera so Frank can see who he's dealing with backed by how he fucked with the wrong team. "Your disrespect has killed what you love". Armando said firing a round into Victoria's head snapping her neck from the brute force of the powerful slug breaching her skull pushing her brains and skull out of the other side.

"Oh my God! Dad! Please don't let them kill me!" Priscilla screamed at the top of her lungs witnessing her sister murdered in cold blood. Frank seeing his fair share of murder, is completely shocked, watching his daughter murdered like this.

"You will return the full ten million within twenty four hours or this one right here is next". Armando said aiming his gun at Priscilla who is crying heavy, in fear, her mouth open no sound only heated painful air being sucked in, scared for her life, that is now in jeopardy. "You don't pay, then I will come for you personally, along with anyone with the Coviello name". Armando said ending the call, leaving Frank time to start putting the ten million together.

Tre and the hommies stripped Frank and his goons of their weapons before they exited, leaving him to get money together. For them this is just another day in New York's gang life. TK looked out for them respecting their gangsta and loyalty.

Victoria's body will be left somewhere in the Bronx to make a statement to anyone in the underground world, don't fuck with the cartel or its associates. Armando stepped in as suggested by Hector to make his presence known. Also because they really fuck with TK, because he is loyal and a breadwinner for the cartel.

Within twenty four hours Frank came up with nine pint five million. Armando paid a big rig driver to take the money to Mexico. As for Priscilla, she was set free. Frank was gunned down by Sleepy Cuz and Sheff Da Hommie. Armando paid them well for this. TK replaced the missing five hundred racks, feeling better regaining control over the money and product, no excuses.

The Crown Is Mine

Chapter 22

A week after TK got things situated with the money and product, all was flowing up and down the coast. Hector sent for him, having Salvator picked him up. Salvator didn't say much to why this unexpected trip was arranged. He just went with it good or bad he can't evade Hector's wrath or reach, especially with him having a global presence.

"You know we really have the life most people make movies about. We have the world at our disposal". Salvator said with his glass of Westland Garryana single malt whiskey. Taking a drink looking out the window of the private G4 jet. TK also having his glass half filled with the aged whiskey, enjoying the finer things in life. "We have to always stay ahead with people wanting what we have, like that idiot Don Coviello and his family thinking they could shake you down, without any kick back".

"That stupid mutha fucka cost me money with him jacking my containers". TK said reflecting back to that moment bringing back that anger, he felt right then.

"In the end, he and his family paid the ultimate cost, their lives, which allows you to continue to be in position. Whether the problem is big or small, we check it right then and there, so it doesn't hinder our business in any way". Salvator said, before taking a drink of his fine whisky. Salvator being a punctual yet strict businessman. He like Hector didn't deal with excuses or any type of infringement upon his many businesses or associates. "There is no good business that comes from doing bad business. This is why I'm embraced amongst everyone I crossed paths with. I come with loyalty and honor to the code of the streets and this business we're in". TK said making it clear, he is the only person that represents him, since Salvator is speaking with a subliminal undertone, referring to Suga Baby and Red Rain. He hasn't seen or spoken to either of them in awhile. Both of them changed their phone numbers, falling off the grid to him, the FBI that was in search of them.

They weren't too far off the grid for Salvator or his unlimited resources that tracked them down retrieving them from Compton. Sal was pleased to make this happen for Hector, especially since he has waited for this, since the moment they fucked up at the store, blowing all that was invested to get them out. Their antics has even sparked a investigation by other federal government agencies, wondering who these trained operatives are, and how they were contracted, more important who contracted them. All information they'll never found out, as long as Salvator's associates keep misdirecting them at the agencies. Lucky for TK being a breadwinner or he would be dead and gone, missing so to speak, since he's the one that contracted them, then the breach came from his side, through the women he loved so much. All this brought on by that small verbal incident that escalated, creating a domino effect of a trail covered in blood and bodies.

"TK your loyalty or way of conducting business has never been in question. This trip is solely because of Hector, Armando and myself see you, your loyalty and what you bring to this organization". Salvator said sipping his whisky then looking out of the window, seeing they're descending onto Hector's private compound. " We're here my friend". Salvator added, before finishing off his glass of whiskey. TK did the same downing it, ready to see what business or problem is at hand. He's thinking, knowing this isn't a leisure trip. The jet touched down, over to the hangar, where they're greeted by a white Jaguar truck, taking them to the mansion. Once the truck stopped they needed to be cleared by Hector's security before they made their way into the large mansion.

"Hermano! In here!" Hector yelled out from the plush living room with cocaine white sofas, statues flowing with the decor, trimmed with 14 carat gold, accented with gold and white marble floor. Soon as they entered TK, he seen Hector playing with his TK junior.

The sight of this sending both joy and pain running through him. At the same time his, mind is in overdrive, knowing Hector has his means and motives behind this move right here.

"He's your twin hermano. May be he will one day take over for you?" Hector said. TK lowering his gangsta shield coming over to pick his son up, showing him fatherly love.

"I miss you little big man". TK said to junior.

145

"Dad dad". Junior said with a smile, never forgetting his father's face. TK's father son moment came to a halt, when he realized this trip with his son being in Mexico, means he knows where Suga Baby and Red Rain are. "Where's his mom and Shandrea? Did you kill them?" TK asked keeping in mind of how much they fucked up for themselves, for him and potential resources. Hector giving off a light laughter before becoming serious. "That wouldn't be good business for me to kill the mother of your child. The women you love. This is why I left this for you to do". Hector responded.

For the first time in doing business with Hector, he felt caught up in a bind that has blind sided him, with this emotionally and mentally crushing task of murdering in cold blood the two women he loves and trust to have his back if shit ever hit the fan. TK's facial expression is displaying his surprise and resistance to the idea itself. TK looked over at Salvator who is preparing himself a drink of cognac from the gold tray in front of him. "Like I said my friend, whether the problem is big or small, you have to check it right then and there". Salvator reiterated to TK.

"I have a lot of respect and loyalty to you Hector and our business arrangement, but putting me in this fucked up position, I'm not feeling it". TK stated looking at Hector then over to Salvator, along with Mexican goons, standing behind the couch he's sitting on, protecting their boss. "How can I look my son in the eyes, knowing I took his mother from him?" TK added standing firm on his decision, love and loyalty for Suga Baby and Red Rain. "Whatever happened to family is everything? Now you're asking me to go against that?" TK added trying get them to see from his perspective, not that they give a fuck. It's all business, and this family of his has cost them all problems, interfering with their business.

Realistically, TK is fully aware if the two women are alive and still here, he nor them will be allowed to leave this large compound, until Hector is satisfied. Hector being informed of all that lead to this very moment.

"It's the smallest things hermano that we overlook that can destroy all we built. The love you have for these women made you go to the extremes to set them free. This love made you ignore how they exposed themselves when they were suppose to be dead to the world. Their actions jeopardized our dark web resources along with all we built. Look at what you went through with the Mafia. It's not good business, because it leads to unnecessary exposure that's all brought on by these two women you love". Hector said, pausing to fire up his cigar, taking a few puffs before continuing. " So hermano do you see why this is necessary?" Hector puffing on his cigar, staring at TK checking his response, because there will be no other way, if he doesn't follow through with this. Hector now standing from the couch, seeing TK is still processing this life changing decision. "Hermano leave your son in here with my staff, while we head out back to take care of what's needed to be done". Hector said. The maid came tending to junior as Salvator, TK and Hector headed out pass the swimming pool area over to the horse stables where there is a dozen stallions Hector and his guest ride. When they entered the stalls, TK seen other Mexican cartel soldiers standing by one of the horse stalls, laughing seeming to be rowdy pointing and laughing at something or someone. When they came up on the stall the soldiers are standing in front of laughing and pointing, there is two other Mexican soldiers holding down Suga Baby and Red Rain trying to have their way with these women they stripped of their clothing leaving them in the nude, not caring about these women, knowing they would be dead soon, so why let it go to waste. They're thinking.

Hector seeing this, became angered and disturbed by it, because he doesn't condone rape or pedophilia, no matter how violent or murderous he can be. Defiling them, living or dead is unacceptable. Hector removing his .40 caliber automatic nickel plated with a pearl handle with the words: Angel De La Muerte Inscribed on it. Meaning: The Angel Of Death. Because when he squeeze the trigger, lives will be taken by the Angels of Death in each slug.

"Que le pasa a pinche ellos!?" Hector snapped asking what the fuck is wrong with them? Before they could turn to his voice, he fired on both of them, killing them with head shoots, slumping their bodies on both women. Both Red Rain and Suga Baby can feel the warmth of the Mexican soldier's bloods spewing on them. "You fucking clowns standing around laughing like this shit is funny, or how I run my business!?" Hector snapped turning his weapon on the other soldiers that should have been watching the women. Instead, they were all taking turns trying to defile them, while laughing about it. Hector's soldiers that accompanied him, now on guard in case they're given the order to gun their fellow soldiers down for going against the rules. TK is gritting his teeth looking over at the women, having conflicting thoughts and emotions, with seeing them being fondled and attempted rape, made him pissed, yet he's task with taking them away from all that pain and humiliation.

"Lo siento jefe". The soldier quickly apologized in fear he would be killed too. Hector now realizing even more how much chaos these two women have caused even now with his men he had to kill. They were good soldiers that just fucked up, going against his code of business and ethics.

Suga Baby and Red Rain having wiggled from underneath of the dead Mexican solder's bodies, seeing TK which is making them feel safe now. "Untie us babe". Suga Baby said looking on at TK, seeing this look on his face that didn't show any promise or way out of this current situation they're in. TK remained silent, truthfully without words, knowing he's seconds away from being forced to kill them.

"Amigo, their lives will live on through your memories of them, and your son. Right now, it's time to get rid of them". Hector said ready to put this all behind him, so they can focus back on business. He turned to his soldier standing their with the M-16 in hand, with .45 Desert Eagle as his side arm. "Oye dame pistola". Hector said to the soldier. The soldier did just that, giving the boss his gun. He handed the gun to TK. TK having a thousand thoughts, one of them is trying to shoot his way out, saving his women and son, but how far would he make it, with the hundred plus Mexican goons on and around the compound. He even thought about offering himself for

149

their lives. "There is no other way out of this hermano. You kill them, we continue business and you can be a father to your son, instead of you all dying and your son being raised here with me". Hector said still holding his gun in case TK shifted his. Love is the most powerful emotion in the world leaving TK in a tormenting state, having to be cornered with this task of killing the two women he loves to save him and his son, otherwise they all die. TK came up on both women leaning in kissing Suga Baby's forehead then her soft lips, just as he remembered them. The kiss also keeping their love alive. He shift his attention to Red Rain finding her soft lips, at the same time pressing the gun to her heart pulling the trigger. Her mouth opened sucking in her last breath, pulling back from the kiss looking into his eyes, still loving him in her last moment knowing he has to sacrifice them to save junior.

Suga Baby seeing and hearing him shoot her girlfriend and love Red Rain, she started screaming in pain with this emotional loss.

"Noooo! Nooo! Don't do this to us! TK please look at me. I love you and our son, please don't do this! Can I at least see my son one more time please, please don't do this!" Suga Baby pleaded.

"Hermano!" Hector called out to TK. He turned to Hector coming over to him, leaving Suga Baby to cry and plead.

"I'm about to finish it". TK said hoping Hector isn't going to make any changes that would hinder his son or make things harder. Meaning obliging her request to see junior. A child will never forget that level of trauma. "You have proven yourself hermano, understanding and honoring what we have. So you don't have to kill her, you can be a family now ". Hector said knowing Red Rain is the one who physically started the problem, with her gone, Suga Baby will be more incline to tone her ways down. This has also lift a weight from TK with not having to kill his son's mother.

Salvator on the other hand, didn't agree with Hector, thinking he mysteriously found a soft spot for this broad who partook in the chaos. A soft spot is a sign of weakness in Salvator's eyes.

"Hector, no excuses or weak links". Salvator said coming around TK to close in on Suga Baby, removing his gun to finish her off. The modified .357 automatic with hollow point tips, twelve in the clip, one in the chamber. Salvator taking aim, finger inside of the trigger guard, until Hector put his gun to Salvator's temple.

"I gave him my word for honoring this business code we have. You kill her it makes me a liar and a piece of shit!" Hector made clear, at the same time Salvator knowing how serious he is, and would pull the trigger if need be. Hector's soldiers also taking aim at Salvator seeing their boss making a statement. Salvator set on getting rid of this weakest link, the soft spot and problem to their business.

"Protecting her from death makes you weak amigo.
You know how we feel about weakness in our business. Besides, you know killing me will destroy all you have down to the horses in this barn". Salvator stated, reminding Hector of who he is, how valuable he is

around the world, being globally connected from underground to governments.

People who have his best interest, with him being a asset to the top political figures, global billionaires, Russian Mafia, Asian Triad and more. Salvator, has brushed shoulders and dined with people that has insured his existence, with the Intel he retains. Anyone killing him will be a target under the assumption they extracted valuable information from him.

"Lower your gun puta, you not going to make me a liar". Hector said still standing firm with his gun to Salvator's temple.

"Okay, okay, if this is how our business ends, I'll lower my gun". Salvator said lowering his weapon. At the same time Hector lowered his gun, Salvator moved swiftly, taking aim squeezing off four thunderous rounds into Suga Baby's face and body, sucking the life from her flesh. In the same quick motion, Hector raised his gun blowing Salvator's brains out, snapping his neck from the brute force of the .40 caliber slug. As Salvator is falling to the ground, TK emptied the clip into his body assuring his death, for robbing him of the second chance he would have had with Suga Baby.

"That piece of shit don't listen! He fucked up big time!" Hector expressed with anger then added. "Chop his body up and feed him to the pigs. His cell phone destroy it!" It's too late for trying to rid traces of his presence. Salvator always allowed someone to know his current location. Whenever he would leave he would make them aware of this too. The people invested in him kept tabs on him anyway, with or without his permission.

"From this point on I don't want anymore problems from your side of business or we will be done and not how you envisioned it!" He said, knowing the sacrifice he made in keeping his word.

Chapter 23

Close to six months passed by, since the cold blooded murders in Mexico at Hector's mansion. TK is still holding onto their love, yet focused back on this business he doesn't have anymore chances in. Hector having killed Salvator, he's been paranoid awaking each night with gun in hand, expecting repercussion. He's ready no matter what.

TK on the other hand has only one worry, moving this product without any further problems, building his empire with the same drive and focus he had the day he step foot out of prison after doing the ten years. This laser beam focus made him go hard like he was broke and hungry all over again. He reached out to the team he put together, the Harrisburg YGs, the nigga T-Geez from North Carolina, along with the Brooklyn Crip niggas, Sheff Da Hommie and Sleepy Cuz. TK made it known to them, there is plenty of product and money to be made out here as long as they stay focus, with no excuses or obstacles in the way of getting to this paper. After flying city to city checking on his new team, he settled in at his Miami mansion, where his staff is looking after junior while he was gone.

"Where's my little man at?" TK asked Maria the maid.

"I just laid him down for a nap. If you like I can awake him so he can see his daddy. You know how excited he gets around you?" She responded.

"I'll let him sleep for now. Can you bring me the bottle of XO Hennessey and a shot glass please?" TK requested, wanting to unwind, at the same time a mini celebration to himself for rebuilding his team and empire.

"Yes I can do that. Are you hungry, is there any thing else I can help you with?"

"Nah I'm good for now". He responded, taking the remote turning on the flat screen television that's mounted on the wall.

He started flipping through the channels, landing on News Nation, seeing the Breaking News with the caption: CARTEL MASSACRE. He turned the volume up, as he tuned in to see and hear what is being said. At the same time wondering if Hector has went to war with El Lobo out of Tijuana, with him vying for the same power and position Hector has. Images of Hector and Armando popped up on the screen as the female reporter started speaking.

"This just in out of Juarez, Mexico. Notorious Cartel Boss Hector Sanchez along with his number two guy, Armando Osario were violently gunned down amongst the one hundred cartel soldiers all meeting their bullet riddled demise. It's been described that the four hundred acre compound was like a small war zone. Mexican authorities are saying this could be the result of a cartel war between rival organizations seeking power and control over distribution. FBI And Mexican authorities that have been investigating Hector Sanchez, say whoever took him out will be next in power to take over eighty percent of global distribution". Heather Abrams said. The blond reporter with tanned skin, glowing blue eyes, with a welcoming smile. As she finished, the news feed cut to footage of the cartel massacre, displaying the view from a chopper that zoomed in on the carnage of Mexican cartel goons gunned down all over the once secured compound. The video cut to the inside of the mansion, showing Armando and Hector slumped at the dinner table. They too never having a chance to grab their weapons. TK now having tons of raw cocaine with no one to answer to. This is good and bad stress. Good being his own boss. Bad having to find someone he can get a stream of product from if he even continues to be in this business that has it's ups and downs. As these thoughts are entering his mind, he glanced towards the kitchen area, where Maria went to get his bottle of XO Hennessey.

"Maria, I need my Hennessey, this crazy shit got me stressing right now!" He yelled out in need of his cognac to absorb this newly discovered information. TK took the remote, turning the television to the video monitors, showing all of the cameras in and outside of the mansion. He looked in the kitchen where she went to retrieve his cognac. No Maria in sight. His hood instincts kicking in, scanning the split screen with a dozen camera angles. Immediately he noticed all of his Fortress Elite Security team are all gone. What TK didn't realize, these men were recommended to him from Salvator. They are also connected to a network of associates Salvator had interest in. So their abrupt absence is a part of Salvator's insurance and words he made clear to Hector, reminding him of who he is. Salvator's every word came to life when close to thirty trained men stormed his compound with silenced weapons and sniper rifles taking out all of his men without them even knowing what hit them, even Hector and Armando died with the look of shock and surprise on their faces.

Shocked by the presence of these trained killers. Surprised that their time has came to an abrupt end. Even the horses were burned in the stables amongst the cartel soldiers that tried to take cover there when they noticed too late what was happening. Everyone connected to Hector including TK has a contract on them, the moment Salvator was killed. His deep rooted connection was aware of his location that night as well as the people he was going to be in the presence of.

TK ran upstairs to his bedroom fearing shit is about to pop off. He wasn't about to just lay down and die, so he went under the bed retrieving a modified AK-47 with a two hundred round drum. He also grabbed his .44 automatic with extend clip, rhino slugs for pure destruction of all hit with each slug. He put it on his waistline. Right now, he's wishing Suga Baby and Red Rain was here to have his back, giving him a chance of evading this outnumbered and out trained situation. He exited the bedroom making his way to junior's room. He's not inside as Maria made him aware of. How did they get to my son? He's thinking. Suddenly, he caught movement out the corner of his eye. He turned quick with his finger inside the trigger guard, pressing up against the trigger, unleashing a barrage of slugs, tearing chunks of the wall by the top of the stairs, forcing whoever it is back.

"I see you mutha fuckas! I know what y'all did to Hector and Armando! I ain't going out that easy! I'm taking somebody with me!" TK yelled out, pumped up with the amount of adrenaline streaming through his body, knowing the end is near. His breathing is heavy as silence fell on the mansion, he's trying to listen in, to see if he can hear any movement that would give him direction on their entry or current position.

Nothing. Only sound he can hear is his heavy breathing and heart thumping. The bedroom door is open, in case he has to take cover. At the same time he's watching the windows and balcony because he's not going out like Montana. He plans on killing anyone moving towards him, squeezing the trigger until the two hundred rounds are gone. Taking somebody with him as he promised. As he's looking into the bedroom towards the balcony, he can see something flying through the air coming from his left side. He turned quick, seeing a small canister dropping to the floor. It didn't register to him what exactly it is. Making it too late for him to respond as he should have, taking cover in the bedroom. Instead the flash bang ignited, jolting and blinding him long enough for the elite men to move in with trained precision, squeezing off, hitting him with center mass shots to the heart, even rushing in on his falling body, double tapping, firing into his face to assure the contract has been fully fulfilled. The contracted men even killing TK's son, covering his head with a plastic bag, suffocating him until his crying could no longer be heard. Even in death, the globally connected Salvator Aielo has a power far greater than anyone could ever imagine, giving him the crown TK has chased down, wearing it for years until the moment of his unexpected graphic demise, erasing his legacy as he once envisioned it.

(THE END)

GOOD 2 GO PUBLISHING CATALOG ORDER FORM

To order books, please fill out the order form below (Please allow up to 2 weeks for shipping)
Make checks payable to: Good2Go Publishing P.O Box 758, Laveen, AZ 85339

Name: _____ Address: _____ City: _____

State: _____ Zip Code: _____ Phone: _____ Email:

Item Name	Price	Qty	Amnt
48 Hours to Die – Silk White	$15.00		
A Hustler's Dream – Ernest Morris	$15.00		
A Hustler's Dream 2 – Ernest Morris	$15.00		
A Thug's Devotion – J.L. Rose	$15.00		
Affliction – Assa Raymond Baker	$15.00		
Affliction 2 – Assa Raymond Baker	$15.00		
All Eyes on Gunz – Warren Holloway	$15.00		
All Eyes on Gunz 2 – Warren Holloway	$15.00		
All Eyes on Gunz 3 – Warren Holloway	$15.00		
All Eyes on Gunz 4 – Warren Holloway	$15.00		
Betrayal Within – Ernest Morris	$15.00		
Black Reign – Ernest Morris	$15.00		
Bloody Mayhem Down South – Trayvon Jackson	$15.00		
Bloody Mayhem Down South 2 – Trayvon Jackson	$15.00		
Business Is Business – Silk White	$15.00		
Business Is Business 2 – Silk White	$15.00		
Business Is Business 3 – Silk White	$15.00		
Cash In Cash Out – Assa Raymond Baker	$15.00		
Cash In Cash Out 2 – Assa Raymond Baker	$15.00		
Chi City Boyz – Asia Hill	$15.00		
Childhood Sweethearts – Jacob Spears	$15.00		
Childhood Sweethearts 2 – Jacob Spears	$15.00		
Childhood Sweethearts 3 – Jacob Spears	$15.00		
Childhood Sweethearts 4 – Jacob Spears	$15.00		
Connected To The Plug – Dwan Williams	$15.00		
Connected To The Plug 2 – Dwan Williams	$15.00		
Connected To The Plug 3 – Dwan Williams	$15.00		
Connected To The Plug 4 – Dwan Williams	$15.00		
Connected to the Plug 4 – Dwan Williams	$15.00		
Cost of Betrayal – Warren Holloway	$15.00		
Cost of Betrayal 2 – Warren Holloway	$15.00		
Death by Association – Ernest Morris	$15.00		
Death by Association 2 – Ernest Morris	$15.00		
Dreams Life – Assa Raymond Baker	$15.00		
Dreams Life 2 – Assa Raymond Baker	$15.00		
Flipping Numbers – Ernest Morris	$15.00		
Flipping Numbers 2 – Ernest Morris	$15.00		
Forbidden Pleasure – Ernest Morris	$15.00		
He Loves Me, He Loves You Not – Mychea	$15.00		
He Loves Me, He Loves You Not 2 – Mychea	$15.00		
He Loves Me, He Loves You Not 3 – Mychea	$15.00		
He Loves Me, He Loves You Not 4 – Mychea	$15.00		
He Loves Me, He Loves You Not 5 – Mychea	$15.00		
Healing In The Midst of Adversity –Michelle Murray	$15.00		
Killing Signs – Ernest Morris	$15.00		
Killing Signs 2 – Ernest Morris	$15.00		
King of the Night – Warren Holloway	$15.00		
Kings of the Block – Dwan Williams	$15.00		
Kings of the Block 2 – Dwan Williams	$15.00		
Lord of My Land – J.M. Morrison	$15.00		
Lost and Turned Out – Ernest Morris	$15.00		
Love and Basketball – J.L. Rose	$15.00		
Love and Deception – Warren Holloway	$15.00		
Love Hates Violence – De'Wayne Maris	$15.00		
Love Hates Violence 2 – De'Wayne Maris	$15.00		
Love Hates Violence 3 – De'Wayne Maris	$15.00		
Love Hates Violence 4 – De'Wayne Maris	$15.00		
Loyalty to a Gangsta – J.L. Rose	$15.00		
Married To Da Streets – Silk White	$15.00		
Mercenary in Love – J.L. Rose	$15.00		
Mercenary in Love 2 – J.L. Rose	$15.00		
My Besties – Asia Hill	$15.00		
My Besties 2 – Asia Hill	$15.00		
My Besties 3 – Asia Hill	$15.00		
My Besties 4 – Asia Hill	$15.00		
My Boyfriend's Wife – Mychea	$15.00		
My Boyfriend's Wife 2 – Mychea	$15.00		
My Brothers Envy – J. L. Rose	$15.00		
My Brothers Envy 2 – J. L. Rose	$15.00		

Item Name	Price	Qty	Amnt
My Brothers Envy 3 – J. L. Rose	$15.00		
Naughty Housewives – Ernest Morris	$15.00		
Naughty Housewives 2 – Ernest Morris	$15.00		
Naughty Housewives 3 – Ernest Morris	$15.00		
Naughty Housewives 4 – Ernest Morris	$15.00		
Never Be The Same – Silk White	$15.00		
Scarred Knuckles – Raymond Baker	$15.00		
Scarred Knuckles 2 – Raymond Baker	$15.00		
Secrets in the Dark Ernest Morris	$15.00		
Shades of Revenge – Assa Raymond Baker	$15.00		
Shoebox Money – Warren Holloway	$15.00		
Slumped – Jason Brent	$15.00		
Someone's Gonna Get It – Mychea	$15.00		
Stranded – Silk White	$15.00		
Supreme & Justice – Ernest Morris	$15.00		
Supreme & Justice 2 – Ernest Morris	$15.00		
Supreme & Justice 3 – Ernest Morris	$15.00		
Sweet Peas Tough Choices – Silk White	$15.00		
Tears of a Hustler – Silk White	$15.00		
Tears of a Hustler 2 – Silk White	$15.00		
Tears of a Hustler 3 – Silk White	$15.00		
Tears of a Hustler 4– Silk White	$15.00		
Tears of a Hustler 5 – Silk White	$15.00		
Tears of a Hustler 6 – Silk White	$15.00		
The Excitement I Bring – Warren Holloway	$15.00		
The Excitement I Bring 2 – Warren Holloway	$15.00		
The Last Love Letter – Warren Holloway	$15.00		
The Last Love Letter 2 – Warren Holloway	$15.00		
The Panty Ripper – Reality Way	$15.00		
The Panty Ripper 3 – Reality Way	$15.00		
The Serial Cheater – Silk White	$15.00		
The Solution – J. M. Morrison	$15.00		
The Teflon Queen – Silk White	$15.00		
The Teflon Queen 2 – Silk White	$15.00		
The Teflon Queen 3 – Silk White	$15.00		
The Teflon Queen 4 – Silk White	$15.00		
The Teflon Queen 5 – Silk White	$15.00		
The Teflon Queen 6 – Silk White	$15.00		
The Vacation – Silk White	$15.00		
Tied to a Boss – J. L. Rose	$15.00		
Tied to a Boss 2 – J. L. Rose	$15.00		
Tied to a Boss 3 – J. L. Rose	$15.00		
Tied to a Boss 4 – J. L. Rose	$15.00		
Tied to a Boss 5 – J. L. Rose	$15.00		
Time Is Money – Silk White	$15.00		
Tomorrow's Not Promised – Robert Torres	$15.00		
Tomorrow's Not Promised 2 – Robert Torres	$15.00		
Trapped in Love – Ernest Morris	$15.00		
Two Mask One Heart – Jacob Spears & Trayvon Jackson	$15.00		
Two Mask One Heart 2 – Jacob Spears & Trayvon Jackson	$15.00		
Two Mask One Heart 3 – Jacob Spears & Trayvon Jackson	$15.00		
Wife – Raneissa Baker	$15.00		
Wife 2 – Raneissa Baker	$15.00		
Wrong Place Wrong Time – Silk White	$15.00		
Young Goonz – Reality Way	$15.00		
Secrets in the Dark 2 – Ernest Morris (New Release)	$15.00		
Secrets in the Dark 1 – Ernest Morris (New release)	$15.00		
The Danger That Lurks Within – Ernest Morris	$15.00		
When Love Happens – Warren Holloway	$15.00		
The Unexpected – Warren	$15.00		
Finding Her Love – Warren Holloway	$15.00		
Murder and Deception – Warren Holloway	$15.00		
Entanglement – Raymond Baker	$15.00		
The Crown Is Mine. Part I	$15.00		
The Crown Is Mine. Part II	$15.00		
The Crown Is Mine. Part III	$15.00		

NOTE: Please make sure the books you order are accepted we are not responsible for rejected orders.

Total: Shipping (Free) Us Media Mail